# BEST

# EROTIC

# ROMANCE

# BEST
# EROTIC
# ROMANCE

*Edited by*
## KRISTINA WRIGHT

*Foreword by*
## SHAYLA BLACK

Published in the United States by Cleis Press, Inc., 2246 Sixth Street, Berkeley, California 94710.

Printed in the United States.
Cover design: Scott Idleman/Blink
Cover photograph: CP Photo Art/Getty Images
Text design: Frank Wiedemann

First Edition.
10 9 8 7 6 5 4 3 2 1

Trade paper ISBN: 978-1-57344-751-5
E-book ISBN: 978-1-57344-766-9

# CONTENTS

# FOREWORD

Shayla Black

Erotic romance. The words sound divine and naughty. They conjure up images of silk sheets, heavy breathing, steamy nights, damp skin, and pleasure beyond our imagination. But more than that, erotic romance says something about us on a deeper level. It's not just sex. Erotic romance marries our hopes and fantasies, our dreams and desires. Erotic romance opens a gateway to deeper connections to other people through the most physical expression of our bodies.

The stories of erotic romance connect our sexual selves with the romantic in us. From a writer's perspective, it's the marriage of two established genres: romance and erotica. Romance is a genre full of hope and fulfillment. We read it in hopes of finding our perfect mate, our very best tomorrows, and the rich emotional lives we'd like to lead. Romance is a journey about people finding one another. It's a fantasy that teaches us that no matter how dire the circumstances, true love wins out. It's the reader's path to believing that everyone has a destined someone and no one will be forever alone.

Classic erotica is one person's journey to self-fulfillment through sexual expression and exploration. Trying new things with new people to create new boundaries and norms is what makes erotica so appealing. Every scenario is open to interpretation, to emotional expression. The sky—and human experience (with a bit of embellishment for fantasy)—is the new limit.

When we put the two genres together, it creates a reading experience that embraces eternal hope and deep sensuality at the same time. It's the ultimate expression of body and soul together. It's a journey that leads us to both our heart's desire and our self-actualized personal best, all because we expressed our deepest sexual self with the person we love and formed a bond meant to last through either a meaningful encounter or the rest of our lives.

Erotic romance takes us to the deepest part of ourselves, forces us to dig deep and ask what we really want. What are we willing to overcome for sex? For love? For something we've always longed for? It allows us to explore deeper longing, deeper conflicts, and even cross boundaries that we wouldn't cross in real life. It allows us to forget our mundane daily existence.

Join these writers on their journey. Embrace these stories for what they are: a true mirror of our inner needs, our longing to combine souls, to discover our truest selves. Explore. Fantasize. Wonder. Romance opens worlds for us. It teaches us to reach for what seems too far away. Enjoy the fight, the conflict, the growth of these characters. Romance is often called a flight of fancy, a genre in which to lose oneself, but there is a truth to romance that serves the greater good. We need to escape our day-to-day lives. We need our happy endings. We need to believe that we can be complete. Join us on this journey and let your fantasies feed a deeper truth. We are not alone. We are only whole when we truly love both ourselves and another human being.

And the journey never ends…Enjoy.

# INTRODUCTION:
## SIMPLY THE BEST

What does it take to be the best? That's the question I kept in the forefront of my mind as I edited *Best Erotic Romance*. And so, when I sat down to sift through the submissions, I found myself reading many of the stories two or three times. It's a complicated process, trying to determine what makes a story the very best of the genre. Obviously, excellent writing and storytelling are key, but I also looked for stories with characters I could believe in and root for. Characters I could fall in love with, just as they were falling in love (or finding ways to stay in love).

I am delighted to present this inaugural collection of *Best Erotic Romance,* the collection that I hope will set the bar for future editions. These are the stories that touched my heart and ignited my libido, that made me think about the nature of desire and the unpredictability of the human heart. Each of these seventeen stories weaves love and passion so tightly that one cannot be separated from the other. And isn't that what a lasting relationship is all about? The need for connection and commitment, memories and history—and hot, wanton, uninhibited sex with a partner who knows us better than we know ourselves.

From tales of love (and lust) at first sight, such as Delilah Devlin's "Drive Me Crazy" and Nikki Magennis's "Dawn Chorus" to stories of established couples still passionate for each other, such as Andrea Dale's "Memories for Sale" and Kate Pearce's "Cheating Time," the stories in this collection show that true love lasts, real passion never waivers, and lovers who are meant to be will always find their way back to each other. These lovers aren't afraid of going after what they want, whether it's long-lost love in "Blame It on Facebook" by Kate Dominic or a hot threesome between a married couple and a female friend in Erobintica's "Till the Storm Breaks."

The authors in this collection know that opening one's heart comes with great risks and often greater rewards and that open communication and a spirit of adventure can make for a scorching sex life. They have created characters who believe all is fair in love and war and who take no prisoners in their quest for emotional and sexual fulfillment. Here you will find lovers exploring their desires in bedrooms, heating things up in the kitchen, splashing around in the bathtub, playing with sex toys, drinking champagne, getting it on in hotel rooms, staying warm in winter cabins, flirting in trucks and bars, making out in the great outdoors, and making love at dawn and midnight—all in the name of that greatest of all human desires: true love.

So, dear reader, I invite you to explore this delicious collection of erotic romance selected especially for you. I think you will find that what makes a story the best of its kind is the same intangible that makes people fall in love. It's magic, I think. And when it comes to love and war, there's only one thing I know for sure: love wins. Love *always* wins.

Kristina Wright
In love in Chesapeake, Virginia

# WHAT HAPPENED IN VEGAS

Sylvia Day

It was 115 degrees in Las Vegas, but Paul Laurens could have sworn the temperature dropped from the chill in his former lover's gaze.

Robin Turner entered the Mondego Hotel's ground-floor lounge like a gust of arctic air. Her long blonde hair was restrained in a sleek chignon and her lush body was encased in a pale blue dress that wrapped around her curves and tied at the waist. Nude-colored heels gave the impression that she was barefoot, while a chunky aquamarine necklace circled her throat like ice cubes.

Paul's grip on his beer bottle tightened and his dick thickened in his jeans. How they'd ended up in bed together was still a mystery to him. One minute they were riding the same elevator and the next he was riding her, the attraction so fierce and immediate he couldn't remember how they reached his room or even shed their clothes.

Taking a long pull on his beer, his gaze followed Robin's progress across the barroom. She approached a booth where a guy in a suit stood to greet her. The man kissed each of her cheeks before they sat. Paul knew he couldn't stay in the same room with her and not have her, so he gestured for the bartender and ordered a martini extra-dirty to be sent to her table.

"Your brews are popular," one of the cocktail waitresses said as she collected the drink and placed it on her tray. Her smile was an invitation. The way she looked him over made sure he got the message.

"I'm glad to hear that," he replied, breaking eye contact to convey his lack of interest. Convincing the Mondego to carry his microbrews had been his first toehold in Vegas. The resort's contract funded his biweekly trips to pitch his product to other establishments in the area, which in turn had allowed him to have Robin for a year. His weekends with her had been the most valuable and treasured blocks of time in his life.

Until four months ago, when he'd fucked up and lost her.

Tossing some bills on the bar, Paul vacated his barstool and carried his beer out to the elevators. He'd left flowers for Robin with the front desk, along with his room number in a note. Although he knew she must have checked in yesterday, she hadn't contacted him. He'd tried to convince himself that she was busy getting ready for the jewelry trade show that opened today in the hotel, but that look she'd just shot him proved the lie. His only consolation was that she wasn't indifferent to him. He could only hope that meant she wasn't totally over him. He'd take whatever he could get from her right now—an argument, a slap to the face, anything at all. As long as it gave him the opportunity to say what needed to be said.

He was stepping into the elevator when he smelled her. Inhaling deeply, Paul pulled the fragrance of vanilla and some-thing flowery deep into his lungs. Awareness sizzled down his spine and fisted his balls, his dormant sexual needs stirring after months without her. He hit the button for his floor, then moved to the back of the car and turned around. As Robin took up a position beside him, anticipation thrummed through his veins. He briefly wondered what excuses she'd made to her companion, then he pushed the thought aside. He didn't give a shit. The only thing that mattered was that she'd followed.

An elderly couple and three suit-clad gentlemen entered the car and faced the doors. As the elevator began its ascent, Robin balanced on one stiletto, drawing Paul's gaze. He watched as she pushed her underwear down, pulling one leg free and then the other.

*Jesus.* His dick throbbed with eagerness and fantasies of stepping behind her, lifting her dress, and pushing into her right there filled his mind.

A soft ding signaled the first stop. The businessmen got off and four teenagers in bathing suits got on. Training his gaze straight ahead, Paul reached over and slipped his hand inside the overlapping front of Robin's dress. She sidestepped closer, putting him slightly in front of her, inviting his touch. He cupped her baby-soft hairless pussy, his fingers curling between her legs and finding her hot and damp. His dick swelled further, and he finished his beer to hide a telling groan.

The car stopped again and the elderly couple exited. As the teenagers moved out of their way, the lone girl in the group glanced at Paul. Interest flared in her kohl-rimmed dark eyes. She checked him out, reading his brewery's logo on his T-shirt and eyeing the tattoo that peeked out from beneath the sleeve. She was following the line of his arm down to where he was parting the lips of Robin's cunt when the two boys with her spread out in the absence of the couple and cut off her view.

Robin sucked in a sharp breath when he pushed his middle finger inside her. Her tight, plush sex sucked at him greedily, and his eyes grew heavy-lidded, lust riding him hard. Pressing his heel to her clit, he massaged her, getting her ready for the pounding drives of his cock. He'd meant to talk with her first, but she was hot for it and God knew he was hot to give it to her. Stumbling through his life without her had been torture. At times, he thought he'd go insane from the need to hear her voice and feel her body against his.

The kids stepped off at the next stop. The car continued its ascent to the forty-fifth floor with only the two of them on board.

"I've missed you," he said gruffly.

In answer, she thrust her desire-slick pussy into his hand. "You've missed this."

Her cool voice sliced into him, but her body betrayed her. She was scorching hot and delectably wet. As he finger-fucked her juicy cunt, soft sucking noises filled the car. Her composure lost, she gripped the brass handrail and moaned, shamelessly widening her stance.

The moment the car reached his floor, Paul pulled his fingers free and caught her up, tossing her over his shoulder and dropping his empty bottle in the trash can conveniently placed just outside the elevator. He had a condom between his teeth and his keycard in hand before he reached his suite. Kicking the door open, he propped Robin against the inside of the stationary half of the double-door entrance. His button fly was open before the latch clicked shut.

His jeans dropped to the entryway's tile, the weight of his chained wallet hitting the floor with a *thud*. A moment later, her lacy underwear fell from her fingers and fluttered down. As he sheathed his cock in latex, Robin pulled her dress up to take him. Paul paused to look at her, his chest tightening. She was unruffled elegance above the waist and a walking wet dream below it. Her legs were long and lithe, her sex pouty and glistening.

He'd been dead when she came into his life, frozen in grief over the death of his son and the subsequent dissolution of his already-broken marriage. That first elevator ride with Robin had been like a flipped switch, jolting him out of his coma. She'd forced the air back into his lungs and the blood back through his veins. He had begun to live for the weekends he spent with her, craving her laughter and smiles, her touch and her scent.

But when she'd suggested they take their relationship to the next level, he had panicked, prompting her to walk out on him with her head held high and his heart in her hands.

Reminded of how damned lucky he was to have her ready and willing again, Paul pinned her slender body against the door and took her mouth in a lush, hot kiss. His lips sealed over hers, his tongue gliding along the lower curve before slipping inside. She was stiff at first, resistant, which got his guard up. When it came to physical intimacy, they'd never had any barriers between them.

As he stroked his tongue along hers, Robin reached for his cock and slung one leg around his waist. She jacked him with both hands, making him so hard and thick he groaned into her mouth and slickened her fingers with pre-cum. She used him to prime herself, massaging the tiny knot of her clitoris with the head of his dick. Impatient, he brushed her hands aside and tucked his cockhead into her slit. She was so ready, he slipped through her wetness and sank an inch inside her. As her cunt fluttered around him, his chest heaved with the loss of his control. What he wanted was to nail her to the door with pounding thrusts; what she needed was to know that he was committed to making their relationship work.

"Hurry," she hissed.

Before he could rein himself in, her hands gripped his ass and yanked him into her. The unexpected thrust sent him tunneling deep. His palms hit the door on either side of her head and a curse burst from his lips.

"Robin, baby," he growled. "Give me a damn minute."

But she was already coming. With her head thrown back against the door and a purely erotic moan of pleasure, her cunt tightened around his aching dick like a tender fist. When the delicate muscles began milking his length in incredible ripples, he lost it.

"Ah, shit," he gasped, feeling his balls tighten and semen rush to the tip of his cock. Gripping her ass in the palms of his hands, Paul fucked her convulsing pussy like a mad man, banging her with hammering strokes. The violent orgasm was the rawest of his life, the pleasure so pure and hot he couldn't stop the growls that tore from his throat. Or the words. "Robin...fuck...I love you, baby. Love you..."

Dripping with sweat and shaking, he sagged into her as the white-hot ecstasy eased, his hips grinding mindlessly as he emptied himself inside her.

She shuddered in his arms and a soft sob escaped her. "God... You're an ass, Paul. You know that?"

*Fucking brilliant.* He finally told her how he felt and it lacked all grace or romance. She'd walked away thinking he just wanted to get laid, and he'd hardly redeemed himself by cursing out his feelings in the middle of a full-throttle, no-preliminaries screw that had probably been heard by every guest on the floor.

His forehead touched hers.

Her arms fell to her sides, her exhales gusting over the perspiration-damp skin of his throat. "I have to go."

Paul's gut knotted. He couldn't let her walk out again. He wouldn't survive it a second time. Gripping her behind the thighs, he hefted her up and kicked free of his boots and wide-legged jeans. In just his socks and shirt, with his dick still hard and buried in the sweetest pussy in the world, he carried her to the bedroom on shaky legs. "Not until you hear me out."

"I heard you loud and clear the last time."

Gritting his teeth, he pulled free of her and dropped her on the bed. Before she could scramble away, he caught her ankles and lifted her legs high and spread them wide. He looked down at her succulent pink pussy, the plump folds glistening with her desire. "I wasn't done. I'm not done."

"*I'm* done."

He licked his lips, hungry for the taste of her. "We'll see about that."

Recognizing the intent in Paul's hazel eyes, Robin struggled to back away before he destroyed her again. She loved a man who was damaged. She could work with that if Paul wanted to heal, but he didn't. The look on his face when she'd suggested they rendezvous in his hometown of Portland had told her all she needed to know—she was his biweekly screw, his hot piece in Vegas. And everyone knew what happened in Vegas stayed in Vegas.

She'd walked out of his hotel room that night with the intention of not looking back. She had told herself Paul Laurens was just a brief spate of madness in her life. But watching him leave the bar just now had been too much for her. She'd left her brother at the table without a word, chasing a man she couldn't recover from.

*One last screw,* she'd told herself. And then it would be over.

Idiot. She craved him like a junky, and one fix was never enough.

Paul sank to his knees between her legs, and her womb clenched greedily. Her pussy trembled with its eagerness to have his mouth on her; her clit throbbed with the need to feel his tongue stroking over it. He held her open with his hands on the backs of her thighs, his gaze riveted to her intimate flesh.

"I've been dying to eat you," he said gruffly. "I've jacked off a dozen times thinking about it. Get comfortable, baby. We'll be here awhile."

"I have meetings to attend!" she protested. "I can't—oh, god!"

The first stroke of his tongue stole her wits. It was a soft, slow lick that fired every sensitive nerve ending. The next pass was more deliberate, working her clit with the ball of his barbell piercing. His groan vibrated against her, making her pussy spasm in want of his cock to fill it.

Her hands fisted the comforter.

"You're so sweet," he praised hoarsely, his hands sliding down to her inner thighs. "Your cunt is so soft."

A soft noise escaped her.

His mouth sealed over her clit in a heated circle, his pierced tongue fluttering over the hard knot with devastating strokes. Her hips moved without her volition, thrusting and rocking as she chased another orgasm. In her past, she'd been lucky to come once with a partner. With Paul, the more he touched her, the more sensitized she became. Each climax came quicker than the one before it until she was coming in rolling waves that seemed to have no end or beginning.

"Fuck me with your tongue," she gasped, draping one leg over his powerful shoulder to urge him closer. Her back arched as he obliged her, teasing her quivering slit with shallow thrusts. Gripping his overlong hair, she rode his mouth, shameless in the extremity of her need.

She'd watched people dismiss Paul out of hand because of his appearance. Those who clung to stereotypes saw mobile homes and biker gangs when they looked at him. They couldn't see past the stubble-shadowed jaw and visible tattoos. But beneath the body jewelry, ink, and shaggy hair was a gorgeous face that was classical in its lines and features. Paul could have graced an ancient coin or inspired a statue in a temple, and he was far wealthier than people would ascertain from his laid-back style.

Cupping her buttocks, he lifted her hips and tilted his head. His tongue pushed deeper, and her pussy clutched helplessly around the rhythmic impalement.

Robin squeezed her aching breasts inside her bra, pinching her nipples to ease their tightness. Her hips churning restlessly, she begged, "Make me come."

Latching on, he kissed her pussy, drawing softly with gentle suction while he rubbed her clit with his tongue. She cried out and fell apart beneath his avid and tender mouth, her body melting into a boneless, breathless, teary puddle on his bed.

"I love you." He pushed to his feet and tossed the condom in the trash.

"You love fucking me," she whispered, knowing that when the passion was sated and reality intruded, he would withdraw again as he'd done before.

Paul leaned over her, pressing his hands into the mattress on either side of her waist. "I'm in this for the long haul."

"You think same time, same place, two weeks from now is a commitment?" She hated the tinge of bitterness in her voice. He'd never made her promises, never alluded to more than what they had during their Vegas liaisons. It wasn't fair that she was angry at him for not giving her more, but she couldn't help how she felt.

"That's not enough for me." Straightening, he yanked his T-shirt over his head. Her eyes swept hungrily over his torso, admiring the tight lacing of abdominal muscles that flexed as he moved. He was so virile. Truly breathtaking. Tattoos covered both of his arms from shoulder to elbow in gorgeous half-sleeves. His chest was broad, golden, and bare...except for her name, which crossed the pectoral over his heart. "It was never going to be enough."

Robin sucked in a tremulous breath, stunned by the sight of ink that hadn't been there previously. Her gaze rested on the new tattoo, her vision blurring with tears. "Paul..."

"I do love fucking you." He pulled a fresh condom out of the nightstand drawer and rolled it on. "When I'm not inside you, I'm thinking about it."

Setting his hands on her inner thighs, he pushed into her. She whimpered, her tender pussy tightened by her recent orgasms.

"God, you feel good," he breathed. "I've needed you so much."

His size, so long and thick, was perfect. As if he'd been made for her. Pushing onto her elbows, Robin watched his glistening cock pull free. The heavily veined length was as brutal looking as the rest of him. The sight of it turned her on further. It made her feel powerfully feminine, like a freakin' sex goddess, to incite the raging lust of a man who was so potently masculine and primal in his sexuality.

Robin's tongue traced the curve of her lower lip. "Please," she whispered, feeling empty without him. She'd been feeling empty since she walked out on him, physically and emotionally.

He sank back into her with a low hiss of pleasure. "You're so sexy, baby. So damn perfect and beautiful. I have no fucking idea what you're doing with a guy like me, but I'm grateful. Every damn day."

God help her. She loved him so much.

He tugged the tie at her waist and pushed the two halves of her dress open. He released the center clasp of her bra, freeing her breasts into his waiting palms. Her pussy tightened around him, echoing the gentle rolling of her nipples between his talented fingers.

"I'm so sorry." He was flushed and shiny with sweat, his beautiful hazel eyes as red as hers felt. "So damn fucking sorry that I ever let you think, for even a moment, that you were nothing but a convenient piece of ass to me. I loved you the moment I saw you. I should have told you—"

"I need things from you." She wrapped her hands around his wrists, anchoring herself as the pleasure threatened to sweep her away.

"I know." His hips rocked in a slow and easy tempo. "I need things from you, too."

That caught her. She wanted him to need her. She wanted to be valuable to him, to serve a purpose in his life. To share his life. "Such as?"

"I need your travel schedule." His lips kicked into a smile when she scowled. "So I can plan my trips to match up with yours. And I need you to move in with me. Your jewelry business is you, right? You can design your pieces anywhere?"

Robin nodded, unable to speak while he was saying everything she'd longed to hear and fucking her so perfectly. The fluid, rhythmic plunges of his cock were driving her half out of her mind. Her entire body was straining with the need to come, her hips lifting to meet his downstrokes. He was so hard and it felt so good to be with him again. To smell the scent of his skin and feel his flesh beneath her hands.

"I'm stuck for now with the brewery in Portland." His words slurred slightly as the pleasure built for him, too. "But if you don't like the city or the house or anything, I'll go where you're happy. I just need time, time I don't want to spend without you."

"Harder," she urged, grabbing his taut perfect ass in her

hands. Her neck arched, her head pressing into the bedding as her climax hovered just out of reach. "Fuck me hard."

Gripping her waist, Paul gave her what she needed. His aggressive strokes set her off in a rush.

"I'm right there with you," he groaned, driving powerfully into her. He made that sexy little noise that made her hot, a cross between a grunt and a hum that said more than words how much pleasure she gave him. "Right there...Right. *There*."

His gaze locked with hers as he came, the heady rush of pleasure shared between them.

"I love you," he grated, shaking with the force of his climax.

She couldn't look away, daring to believe.

Paul got her naked. Robin missed how he accomplished the feat while in her euphoric postclimax haze, but she was grateful for the result. She lay curled against his side, her legs tangled with his. Her head lay on his chest and her fingertips tracing her name imprinted in his skin.

"I was going to fuck you and walk out," she confessed.

"I caught that." He pressed his lips to her forehead. "I wouldn't have let you leave. I would've followed you with my junk hanging out if I had to and hauled you back."

She lifted her head. "Like I'd *ever* let other women get an eyeful of you."

Paul smiled. "I'm all yours, honey. Flaws, baggage, and all."

Her hand stilled and settled over his heart. "You're not ready, Paul. I wish you were."

"The counselor I've been talking to says otherwise."

Robin's heartbeat skipped. "Counselor?"

He nodded. "I'll need to keep seeing him for a while, but I know enough about what losing Curt did to me to have my head on straight again."

Her heart ached for the tragedy he'd suffered. She couldn't imagine what it would feel like to outlive your child.

His fingers linked with hers. "I should have talked to someone a lot sooner, most especially after I started seeing you. It wasn't fair to you that I didn't."

"You can't take all the blame," she said softly. "When we started out, our arrangement was perfect for me, too. No strings, hot sex, and a guy who listened to me ramble on about jewelry. Things were fine until I changed my expectations."

He reached over with his free hand and opened the nightstand drawer. She thought he might be reaching for a condom, and her pulse quickened. Then a dark blue velvet box appeared in her line of vision, and her heart stopped altogether.

Paul set the box on his washboard abs and took a deep breath. "Do you have any idea how hard it is to buy an engagement ring for a jewelry designer who's kicked your ass to the curb?"

Unable to help herself, she reached for the box.

"Wait," he said, staying her. "Going back to the list of things I need from you...I need you to marry me, Robin. The next time we leave this room, I want us to come back to it as man and wife. I promise you'll have the wedding of your dreams, with our friends and family and doves and swans and whatever the hell you want, but I'd really like the vows now—today—and getting married here in Vegas feels like it fits us."

*Us.* She looked at him with wide eyes, her mind telling her how crazy that was. There were so many courtship steps they were skipping. What they'd had in their year together—not counting the four miserable months apart—was emails, phone calls, six days a month of the hottest sex of her life...

...and a sharp, pure feeling of connection that had hit them both like lightning the moment they'd laid eyes on each other.

"I know it's crazy," he said, reading her mind, as he so often did. "But we've been crazy over each other from the start. I'm lovesick over you, baby. I swear you'll never regret taking a chance on me. I'll make you happier than you've ever been in your life."

Swallowing hard, she thumbed open the box.

"Oh, Paul," she breathed, her fingers shaking.

"Do you like it?" His rich, deep voice was laced with a rare note of anxiety. "We can exchange it if you don't. You can pick out whatever you want. Something more traditional maybe—"

"Shut up." The ring was perfect. It was unusual, almost quirky, with a massive diamond—around four carats was her educated guess—surrounded by irregular swirls of multisized rubies.

"When I look at it," he said quietly, "it reminds me of how I feel about you."

She saw that in the ring, too. The unusual design conveyed passionate chaos, and the fact that he registered that quality in the setting cemented her belief that he was the perfect man for her.

Climbing over him, Robin straddled his hips and extended her hand. "Put it on me."

The feel of the cool band sliding over her knuckle was so sublime it caused goose bumps to sweep across her skin. She wanted this so badly, wanted *him*. Her rough-edged brewmaster with his gentle hands and insatiable hunger for her body. The man who listened to her talk about gem clarity and design theory and who patiently explained the difference between lager and ale.

"Yes," she answered him, placing her hand on his chest next to her name over his heart.

Paul framed her rib cage with his hands, his thumbs stroking the lower curve of her breasts. "And what do you need from me?"

"I needed this." She gestured between them. "A commitment from you. I'll also need a room that's mine alone, a workshop with lots of light and space."

"Done."

"And I need you to promise not to change your style for me."

His brows rose. "I have a style?"

"I love you just the way you are. Don't cut your hair or—"

He rolled abruptly, taking the top. "Say that again."

Laughing, Robin looked up into his impossibly handsome face. "Don't cut your hair?"

He snorted. "The part before that."

"Don't change your style?"

Bending his head, Paul caught her nipple between his teeth. She made a soft noise at the unexpected bite, then arched her back when his tongue soothed the slight sting. When his cheeks hollowed on a drawing pull, she moaned his name and gave him what he wanted.

"I love you, Paul. You're everything to me."

When he lifted his head, the fiercely tender look on his face was one she'd remember for the rest of her life.

Or she could just make him show it to her again. She had a lifetime to work on it.

# FIRST NIGHT

Donna George Storey

It was a mistake.

Sophie gazed at Justin's sleeping face, so pale against the pillow in the dawn light. Her chest tightened. He was even more beautiful when she could stare to her heart's content at his thick lashes, the artful slope of his nose, the luscious curve of his shoulder.

Yes, he was gorgeous, but it was still a mistake.

Sophie glanced over at the alarm clock, which glowed an ice-blue "6:08." In approximately six hours she and this young man were supposed to tie the knot.

But she simply couldn't go through with it.

Her brain ticked off the familiar list: dress, flowers, photographer, ceremony, reception, table assignments, band, cake. This time it wasn't to reassure herself all was in order but rather to calculate the damage, the shocked faces, the dollars lost, when the bride called the whole thing off the morning of the wedding.

Just then, Justin sighed and rolled closer, his hard-on brushing her thigh.

Sophie leaned toward him and inhaled deeply, savoring the scent of his flesh—cream and earth mixed with a touch of cumin. The insistent ache in her belly was her own version of Justin's morning boner, which rose unfailingly each day with the sun. She was tempted to reach down and stroke him, even though she'd been the one to suggest they abstain for a week before the wedding. But now she wanted nothing more than to feel his hard cock inside her.

The problem had nothing to do with Justin himself. It was the stupid piece of paper that would ruin everything.

Suddenly Sophie's lips stretched into grin. Her brain was foggy—she'd barely slept all night—but she might have a solution to the problem after all. Just as planned, she would dress up in her perfect white sheath and glide off to the lovely historical mansion to be photographed and admired. She would float through the flower garden with her attendants to the wedding gazebo and take Justin's arm. And then she would turn and address the assembled guests with the utmost dignity:

"I want to thank you all for coming today. I know the invitations suggested you would be witnessing a wedding ceremony between Mr. Justin Trevor Phillips and myself, but actually, I have another reason for calling you together. I want to announce that I am having really fabulous sex with Justin. It's so great that I tricked myself into thinking I had to marry him to keep having these mind-blowing orgasms for the rest of my life. Now I realize that not only can we keep fucking like wild animals without the benefit of a stupid piece of paper, but statistics suggest that we'll have better sex without it. But trust me, the kind of bonks Justin and I regularly indulge in are well worth celebrating openly with friends and family. So please enjoy the grilled salmon lunch and the salsa dancing and maybe you can snatch a little afternoon delight yourself in the gardener's shed or the bamboo grove."

Sophie giggled quietly. If only she could be so honest. Honesty was a good thing. Except the kind of honesty she got from her girlfriends at her bachelorette party two nights before.

The ladies were on their second pitcher of sangria when her college roommate, Ashlyn, started in on the topic of married sex.

"Wedding nights sure aren't what they used to be. Sean and I were so exhausted after all the festivities, he could barely haul me over the threshold of the honeymoon suite, and then we both fell fast asleep on this great big fancy bed. Of course, the morning after was all the better since we were so well rested. I love daytime sex, but sometimes I wonder if the nap afterward isn't the best part."

The other women, all except Sophie, chuckled knowingly.

Nina, her best friend all through high school, leaned close. "Sex definitely loses its edge once it's legal, but Jasper and I try to get away for the weekend once a month or so. Then I pretend we're having an illicit affair, and we don't get out of bed until we're chased from the room by the maid."

The other women exchanged sly glances and murmured approval.

"You definitely have to work to keep things spicy," her friend Megan added. "But I really like the closeness, too. Marriage really changed things with Brian. It's funny but we can get buzzed just lying in each other's arms and planning home improvements."

"The real change comes after you have kids. We don't do it nearly as often, and we have to be very quiet, but our bond is deeper, more spiritual," added her other college friend, Jenny. Sophie's older sister, Elena, nodded and smiled.

Sophie, who had been pleasantly buzzed from the wine until a moment before, slumped down in her chair. "Tell me the truth. Am I giving up hot sex forever by marrying Justin?"

"Justin's a great guy, Sophie, you definitely want a commitment so he doesn't slip away," Ashlyn said, her expression solemn. "And there's more to your relationship than sex, right?"

At the time Sophie nodded. Of course there was more to their relationship. They made each other laugh. He cooked a delicious pasta primavera. And there was no place she'd rather be after a rough day at the office than enfolded in his arms. But would any of that have the same glow without frequent refuelings of wild, wet, and very satisfying copulation?

Such thoughts still troubled her as she lay beside her boyfriend, the end of their wonderful sex life just hours away.

As if he somehow sensed her doubts, Justin's eyes fluttered open. He smiled and slipped an arm around her. She snuggled against him, her head resting against his shoulder, their legs tangled together like his signature linguine. She secretly called this position "All is right with the world," because she never wanted anything else when they were floating together like this. Especially after a good round of scream-until-your-throat-is-raw sex.

But, after they were married and stopped having sex, maybe this feeling of contentment would be enough? She started to ask Justin, to tell him of her fears, but his breath had grown slow and even, and she didn't want to disturb his rest. He'd need all the strength he could get later.

When she told him the wedding was off.

After all, what did a stupid piece of paper mean in this day and age anyway?

Maybe that was part of the problem. Deep inside she wanted a traditional wedding night, which meant they would touch each other in a way they had never experienced before. But in the two years they'd known each other, they'd already licked and sucked and penetrated each other's bodies in every way possible. How could they manage anything new or surprising tonight?

It would be so different if they had fallen in love a hundred and fifty years ago, at the height of Queen Victoria's reign. Proper gentleman that he was, Justin would have courted her on countless Sundays after church before he asked her father for her hand. And yes, he'd have whirled her around the dance floor until her bosom was heaving and lifted her from carriages, his strong hands encircling her tiny, cinched waist. All the feelings she had *down there,* beneath her voluminous petticoats, would remain unnamed and unexpressed but in a subtle blush, a catch in her breath when he touched his lips to the back of her hand.

And then, on their nuptial night, the famine of touch would suddenly turn to a free-for-all feast. Justin's tongue would probe her mouth, his hands would caress her tender breasts, his manhood would sink inside her most intimate flesh for the very first time all in the same hour.

How intense was that?

Instead of dragging her off to a tapas bar and a dance club, her dearest girlfriends would attend her in her bridal chamber. They would guide her to the canopied bed, brush her long hair over her shoulders, tuck a fresh rosebud in the neckline of her flowing white nightgown for Justin to remove—literally, deflower—when he claimed his husbandly prerogative. In those days, a man owned his wife's body as completely as he owned land or horses.

Sophie wondered what she would have felt when Justin, her first and only lover, explored all the treasures of his new possession, brushing her sensitive nipples with his fingers, slipping his hand between her nether lips. Would her new husband be gentle or strangely transformed by lust? Would she weep from the total surrender of her heart, her body, her name? Would she cry out when he mounted her, wincing from the pain that was a woman's duty and yet a secret pleasure as well?

Sophie sighed. Justin had been her eighth lover, although he'd been her first for a few of the more esoteric sexual practices most fairly adventurous couples enjoyed on occasion: back-door sex, light bondage, the occasional pearl necklace. Yet the timeless experience she longed for—a first night of profound erotic transformation in the arms of the man she loved deeply—was a pleasure she could never know.

"Hey."

Startled from her Victorian era reverie, she looked up to meet her fiancé's twinkling blue eyes.

"Good morning, Mr. Phillips. You look happy."

"I am. Today's the happiest day of my life."

"Why?" Sophie asked. Still half-lost in her musings, she was genuinely surprised by his answer.

"Silly. Because I'm marrying the most wonderful, beautiful woman in the whole world."

Oh, right, speaking of our wedding...

"Aunt Sophie!" Elena's four-year-old daughter, Madison, burst into the room and rushed over to the bed. "You're getting married today."

"We are. And you're going to be the best flower girl ever," Justin said in the perfect avuncular tone, warm but not condescending. He'd be a great father, Sophie thought with a pang of regret.

"My dress is so pretty. I can't wait to see yours." The little girl was starting to crawl in bed with them when Elena appeared and led her daughter back toward the guest room.

She gave Sophie a sly look. "I hope she didn't disturb you. By the way, Mom and Dad said they'd come over from the hotel by eight. The appointment with the hairdresser is at nine, right?"

"Yeah," Sophie said weakly, that now-familiar dread closing

around her ribcage like a corset. She might not be a real Victorian bride, but apparently her sex life was still to be molded by forces beyond her control.

If she was making a terrible mistake, it was too late to turn back now.

The day went by so fast, Sophie almost forgot she was making a mistake. The wedding ceremony in the garden brought her to tears, but not because she was depressed about the upcoming drought in her bedroom. There was something strangely moving about declaring her love for Justin in front of so many beaming, overdressed people who really seemed to wish them the best in their life together. With the whirl of the reception and the after-party back at the house, the day slipped into evening. It was six o'clock before they managed to drive off to the charming bed-and-breakfast they'd booked for the first night of their honeymoon.

Only then, when Justin scooped her up and carried her over the threshold of their wine country cottage, did she remember this night was the beginning of the end of her erotic life.

Yet, far from being tired or disinterested, Justin immediately deposited her, with a meaningful wink, right in the middle of the four-poster bed. Then he stretched out beside her, pulling her close. "I've been looking forward to this part of the ceremony all day."

"Are you sure you don't want to turn in early? We have the rest of our lives to perform our marital duty."

"Hell, no, not when you made me hold off for a whole week," he blurted out, then remembered his manners. "Sorry, sweetie, I know you didn't sleep so well last night. If you want to go to bed early, it's okay with me," he lied politely.

Although she'd hardly slept, eaten, or drunk anything in the past twenty-four hours, Sophie's body was tingling with a strange excitement. "Well, we're supposed to consummate the marriage as quickly as possible—to make it legal."

Justin frowned. "Speaking of the proper formalities, I wanted to talk to you about something."

Sophie's pulse leaped. The ink on the marriage license was barely dry and things were going sour already. "What is it, honey?"

"I was looking at that checklist from your bride guide this morning, and it said I was supposed to buy you a wedding gift. Pearls or something. I didn't get anything, but if there's something you want…"

"I didn't get you anything either. They recommended cufflinks or a watch for you. Very 1950s." She turned and cupped her hand around the erection tenting his khakis. "But this is something I wouldn't mind getting all wrapped up with a bow."

"It's all yours. If I can have this." He slipped his hand under her going-away skirt and patted her mons. "I promise I'll take very good care of it."

She laughed. "It's a deal."

Justin's fingers began to stroke her through her panties.

"Of course, in the old days, you would have owned me," she murmured, her legs falling open. "And I'd have come to you a virgin. This would be the very first time we did anything but hold hands."

"If this were the first time I was touching you, I'd probably come in my pants just doing this," Justin said softly. With his free hand, he reached over and began unbuttoning her blouse.

"But you wouldn't be a virgin. Your uncle would have taken you to a house of ill repute to break you in. So you could break *me* in."

"I didn't know you were such an old-fashioned girl at heart." Justin finished with the buttons and eased the blouse over her shoulders. Was she imagining a new possessiveness in his touch?

"I'm glad I'm not a virgin," she continued, "but there's still something sexy about having your wedding night be the first time."

He hooked a hand around her bare shoulder and pulled her body toward him, coaxing her to straddle his belly. Unsnapping her bra with an expert hand, he pulled it down over her arms. The steely gleam in his eyes as he stared at her naked breasts was definitely new.

"I'm glad it's not our first time," he said.

"Why?"

Justin looked her straight in the eye, and for an instant Sophie did feel possessed, owned. Yet at the same time her body was strangely free and buoyant.

"Because I know you're going to enjoy it," he said firmly. "I know I'm going to make you come."

"Oh, god," she whispered, a hot wave of arousal fanning up from her pussy up through her chest. Then she cried out again, "Oh, god, sorry about that."

"What?"

"This has never happened before. I sort of, well, flooded my panties. I'm just so...turned on. The way you're talking..."

Justin's finger burrowed under the elastic of her underwear and came out glistening. Smiling mischievously, he anointed her stiff nipple with her own moisture.

She squirmed and bit her lip.

"I see you like it when I talk dirty and rub your own juices on your tits," he said, his voice husky.

Sophie felt another release between her legs. Her arousal had never been so obvious—or copious. "Sorry, again," she stammered, "I think we're both drenched now."

"Then let's get out of these wet things. I want you naked anyway," he replied. There was definitely a new confidence in his tone, as if her obedience was expected and required.

Of course, Sophie wanted to be naked, too. She quickly unfastened her skirt, slithered out of her soaking underwear. Justin was out of his khakis and briefs in record time. With a shiver of embarrassment, she noticed the circle of moisture she'd deposited on his fly.

Her husband pulled her onto his belly again, his hard cock nudging up against her ass. "Now rub your wet pussy against me. Make it happen again."

"I don't know if I can."

"You're my wife now, Sophie. You have to do what I say in bed. And it's not just that piece of paper. You yourself gave me your pussy as a gift. So I want it to drool all over my stomach to show me how turned on you are."

Sophie wanted to do as he asked, but her body's strange new response was really beyond her control. Still, it was her duty to try her best to satisfy her husband's carnal appetites. And so she began to grind her swollen lips against his belly, in an effort to produce another mysterious effusion of desire.

Justin grabbed her ass and squeezed hard. "I like it that you're so horny you have to masturbate on me, but I'm not sure if you're trying hard enough. Do I have to spank you to get you to obey? Now that you're mine, I can punish you when you don't please me."

Sophie stiffened as if she'd actually been struck. In an instant, a fresh puddle of her hot juices pooled onto his belly.

Justin arched back into the mattress. "Fuck, I love that. How do you do that?"

"You're doing it to me. It's you," Sophie admitted.

"You like this, huh?"

"Yes, but I like you inside me even more. Mind if I climb on?"

He'd never turned down such a request before, but tonight Justin merely narrowed his eyes. "Don't you know a proper woman waits for her husband to decide these matters? Besides, when we lie together as man and wife for the first time, you'll be beneath me, where you belong. Do you understand?"

Sophie opened her mouth to protest—where the hell did he get off spouting this patriarchal shit anyway?—but her complaint turned to a helpless whimper as she felt another gush below.

"I understand," she said, her eyes lowered meekly.

"Then lie on your back and bring your knees up to your chest so your sopping pussy will be nice and tight."

Trembling, Sophie complied. She felt so naked and exposed, holding her knees open for him, uncertain what rough, domineering treatment awaited. And yet her body seemed to trust him. Every fiber of her being shivered with delicious anticipation.

Justin knelt between her legs, his eyes surveying her. "I'm going to consummate our marriage now. Then you'll be mine." His tone was gruff rather than loving, but at that moment Sophie felt her chest wrench open, as if he'd reached in and tugged on her heart. As she waited breathlessly, her husband took his dick in his hand and rocked forward. But he didn't slide it in. Instead he pressed the head of his cock against her clit. She moaned. Justin rubbed her with his tool, like a big, swollen finger, claiming her there first. She was so wet, his penis slipped over her slick flesh with a faint, slurping sound.

"Please, take me," she choked out.

On the next stroke, he guided his cock to her hole and buried himself to the hilt.

They groaned in unison.

He began to move, slowly, pressing tight against her to give her the friction she needed.

"You belong to me now and I'm going to make you come," he hissed in her ear.

Another gush of wetness glazed the crack of her ass. Justin's balls slapped against her cleft as he drove into her, stimulating the tender flesh. He took her nipple in his mouth and sucked hard.

*Tying the knot*—those words had scared her, confused her, but that's just how Sophie felt now, deliciously tied and tangled, her legs twisted around his ass, a knot of lust throbbing low in her belly. With each thrust, Justin seemed to push deeper, conquering unknown territory. Because no one had ever touched her this way before, not even the sweet Justin she'd watched sleeping that very morning. No one had ever opened her so completely—her cunt, her heart, her head all at once—to expose yearnings secret even to herself.

"Come for me, Sophie," he panted. "I order you to come right now."

Dutiful wife that she was, she bucked up against him—one, two, three more times—and then she was coming, wracking spasms that burst from her throat in a shriek. Justin planted his hands on the bed and reared up, his hips pounding her like a porn star as he announced his own climax with a series of low grunts.

He fell forward and they clutched each other, their bodies still heaving. They were so close she could feel his heart pounding in her own chest.

"I'm not sure what came over me just now," Justin confessed. "I hope that lord-and-master talk wasn't a mistake."

"No way. I think I left a wet spot on this bed the size of California." She moved her lips to his ear and added in a whisper, "You bossy bastard. That was super hot."

"You're hot, baby. God, I'm lucky. I have the sexiest wife in the world." He rolled onto his back and they snuggled together, her head on his shoulder, their legs twined together.

Sophie smiled. She had made a terrible mistake—spending the whole day worrying her sex life would be ruined by a piece of paper. But tonight she learned it could be a passport to new possibilities.

# ANOTHER TRICK UP MY SLEEVE

Heidi Champa

"Are you sure about this, Daisy?"

"Yeah, I'm sure. Why wouldn't I be?"

His arms were fixed to the bed frame with two old ties, and I was decked out in the vinyl outfit I had hand-picked with his specifications in mind. Now that the moment had finally arrived, he seemed underwhelmed, and I was starting to sweat in the tight-fitting black plastic. He rolled his eyes and sighed, his back collapsing against the bed, his muscles loose. I was starting to get discouraged. But, I pressed on, banging my pink leather riding crop against my open hand. Blake didn't look scared, and there was absolutely no desire in his eyes. My back, which I had been holding straight in an attempt to look authoritative and sexy, started to droop. None of this was going how I thought it would.

"Blake, I thought you were into this, what is the problem?"

He squirmed against his ties, but not in the way I was hoping. He tried to sit up but couldn't, and had to settle for an odd, reclined position that almost made me laugh.

"I don't know Daisy, I just don't really feel like it tonight."

I sat on the edge of the bed and dropped my fetching whip on the floor. My knee-high patent leather boots were staring to hurt my feet, and I felt more ridiculous than I ever had before.

"This is all your fault, you know that Blake!"

"I know, baby. I know."

It was an offhand remark after a silly night of playing the game "I Never" with some friends. It wasn't meant to be an insult, or at least that is what he said after the fact. There was no maliciousness in his words; he'd spoken them matter-of-factly as he pulled the car into the driveway.

"I think our sex life has gotten boring."

I didn't necessarily disagree with him, but I was quick to point out all the crazy things we had done in the past. When we first got together, our nonstop sex sessions were the stuff of legend, and we could hardly keep our hands off each other. I was confident that our sex life was anything but boring. But, Blake was just as quick to point out that our last truly adventurous tryst had been years before. As much as I hated to admit it, the sad fact was, he was right. He stopped short of saying we were in a rut, but I read between the lines. Adventure and lust had been replaced by comfort and our daily routine, which sadly didn't have much room for sex. I always thought it was just a natural part of being together for a long time. I didn't want to admit that I wasn't all that thrilled about our bedroom life either, but in my heart I knew. He didn't say anything more that night, but his words had sent me on a mission. And, that mission was never to be boring in bed again.

Blake didn't know it then, but he had unleashed a monster. I hit every adult toy and video shop in a nearly fifty-mile radius in search of the ticket to sexy, smutty bliss. Books, DVDs, toys; you name it, I bought it. We'd tried more positions from the *Kama Sutra* than I knew existed and came away with more than a few pulled muscles. One position, called the "pair of tongs," nearly put us both in the emergency room.

Some of the toys I picked up scared Blake, but he enjoyed the beautiful glass dildo I purchased almost as much as I did. We rented and watched all kinds of porn, and not just the kind with "women-friendly" plots and stories. Blake was stoked at first and happily shared his love of hot girl-on-girl action with me. But, soon he found that he preferred to watch most of it alone, like he always had before. The DVDs now sat in a pile by the small television on the dresser, neither of us watching them at all.

Our foray into role-playing took longer and didn't really take hold until after a particularly good time at a Halloween party. I had never found Dracula sexy before, but Blake convinced me to join him in my sister's guest room, and he turned me from a sexy kitty to a kitty in heat in no time flat. After that night, I bought more outfits to act out fantasies of all types. I chose the naughty nurse; Blake had a thing for lady cops, which we managed to accomplish with the help of a fake nightstick and the back seat of our car on a deserted dirt road. It had all been passionate and fun and, I thought, completely worth it. There wasn't a boring night of sex in months, and we both seemed to be enjoying the ride.

The dominatrix fantasy was mostly my idea, but Blake seemed more than a little interested. The outfit was the most expensive one yet, but I relished putting it on and the power I felt holding the whip was undeniable. I had hoped that Blake would be a good little submissive, but his willful eyes left me no choice but to reach over and untie him.

"I'm sorry, Blakey. I thought this would be fun, but if you

don't want to do it, maybe we can save it for another time."

After I freed him, I felt even more foolish in my getup than I did before. He rubbed his wrists, and I moved off the bed to change out of my new personae. Blake shook his head and grabbed my arm to pull me back down next to him.

"Daisy, I'm sorry. I really am. But, I don't know. Do you think we could just have sex tonight?"

"We were going to have sex, Blake. That was the point of this whole thing."

He stared at me until I looked up, embarrassment making my cheeks flush.

"No. I mean sex. Like we used to have. Just you and me, on our bed. You know, sex. I hate to use the word *normal,* but it somehow seems appropriate."

"You mean boring sex?"

"God, fuck! I wish I'd never said that. That's what all this has been about, hasn't it? Because I said we were boring in bed."

"No."

Blake didn't say a word, but he made it clear with his eyes that he knew I was lying.

"Okay, fine Blake. Fine. Yes. I was trying to make our sex life less boring. You seemed to enjoy it. What's changed?"

"Nothing. And, I did like most of it. But, I miss being with you. Is it so crazy to want to feel you, be with you and watch you come? No bells, no whistles, no whips. Just you and me."

Secretly, they were the words I wanted to hear since our sexcapades began. I had been afraid to say it, but hearing Blake confess made my resolve melt away.

"If that's what you really want. Who am I to say no to an idea like that?"

Blake stood up, pulling me to my feet with him. He reached behind me and started to unzip my outfit, peeling the black vinyl down my skin until my breasts popped out of the top. As he continued to undress me, he captured one of my nipples in his mouth, swirling his tongue and sucking in a wonderfully familiar way. He released me all too soon, and I helped Blake with the rest of my outfit, stretching it over my shiny boots and tossing it aside. He dropped to his knees and started untying my boots, taking his sweet time, kissing my legs as he went. When he was finished, he sat on the bed, sliding back toward the headboard, the same place he was before I let him loose. He was waiting for me to do something, and I didn't hesitate to oblige him.

I didn't try and come up with something interesting; I just straddled him. My legs wrapping around his waist, I kissed him deeply, rocking slightly on his lap. I felt his bare chest with my hands, the heat coming off his skin in waves. He leaned forward, his tongue flicked over my collarbone, dropping kisses down to my breasts. His fingers teased me, pulling my nipples into tight peaks, while his mouth stayed away, only making me want it more. I arched my back, but he went on with his game. Until I started grinding myself against his growing cock. He then became much more generous with his affection. He mumbled against my skin, the vibration tickling me.

"This is more like it, Daisy. Aren't you glad I finally said something?"

He moved right back to my breasts, not waiting for my response. The heat of his mouth on my nipple made me turn to jelly inside, my body tensing with each sucking kiss. Before I knew it, he flipped me on my back, resuming his torture of my hard nipples with his hands and mouth. I lay on the bed, helpless, letting him slowly circle each nipple with his tongue, drawing me closer and closer to losing my mind. Then, he started sinking lower, his mouth teasing, tickling down my stomach until I was trembling under his lips. I felt his long fingers tracing over my pubic hair, running aimlessly about, avoiding what I really wanted him to do. The lightest pressure of his fingers made me heat up inside, liquefying under his touch. I moved my hips in circles, enjoying the barest of touches. But, I wanted more. I pulled him up so I could look at him, and he was smiling like a very happy boy.

"Blakey, please stop teasing me. I need you."

"Sorry, but it's been a long time since I've gotten to do this. You'll give me a little latitude, won't you?"

He was half on top of me, kissing me deep on the mouth. His fingers danced over my taut nipple, barely grazing over it. His hand seemed so big gripping my hip, pulling me close. My hands cradled his face as I tried to hold on to the moment for as long as I could. I ran my finger over his mouth, and he caught it between his lips, sucking it into his mouth. My stomach rolled over, and a new wash of heat ran through me. His face dropped from my hands, and he kissed down my neck. Every inch of my skin caught on fire, each little kiss, lick starting a new blaze. I clawed at his hair, urging him forward, pushing him further down my body.

But, again, Blake would not be rushed. His mouth again latched on to my nipple, sucking it deep into his mouth, flicking it over and over with his tongue. Arching my back, I tried to get more. All I could think was that I needed more. More of anything that Blake wanted to give to me. The heat of his mouth was joined by his slow, tracing fingers moving up my thigh. I could feel the gentle tremble of my leg under his touch every time he got nearer to my pussy. He seemed to be purposefully avoiding my most sensitive skin, teasing me with little touches everywhere else. He pushed my legs apart, and I felt his fingers moving closer and closer to my cunt. Moans were escaping my throat, his mouth moving back and forth over my nipples, teasing one and then the other until I was ready to scream.

"Blake, I can't take much more of this."

"Just a little bit longer, I promise."

His mouth covered mine, stopping any more words from getting out. His finger had finally found my slick heat, and my hard clit was sliding under his soft touch. The small circles teased my clit until I found my hips moving along, trying to get Blake to go faster. But, he kept going at the maddeningly slow pace, his eyes watching my face.

"God, you are so beautiful when you are excited, do you know that?"

I could only manage to shake my head no, as no words were possible at that moment. His words were tearing at my brain, making my chest flush with renewed heat. His finger slipped down past my clit and entered me, opening my pussy up for the first time. The flat of his palm grazed my clit, with each slide in and out.

"Open your eyes. Please, Daisy, open your eyes."

I could barely stand it, but I did. His green eyes shone back at me, intense and sparkling.

"Blake, please, I need you."

He kissed me, hard and probing, all his energy filling me. Without missing a beat, his face dropped down, sweeping kisses over my quivering hips, down to my open thighs. I felt his breath between my legs, his fingers caressing my lips, sweeping over me. He was just looking at me, taking me in while I was writhing, waiting for his mouth to touch me. I felt the tip of his tongue gently touch my clit, and I felt like my mind was going to come apart. His gentle sweeping strokes covered my pussy, teasing me until I was shaking and clawing at the sheets. The long fingers that I had fallen in love with so long ago were finally touching me, spreading me open, filling my tight pussy, pleasing me. The sensation was so intense, I didn't know if I could handle much more.

He kept slowly teasing me, tasting me, urging my desire forward, pushing me closer to the edge. His fingertip swirled the smallest circles over my clit. I gasped at his masterful touch, the pressure just enough to thrill me but not enough to make me come. His finger slid inside me, my walls gripping him, pulling him deeper into me.

"God, I've missed you like this, Daisy. So much."

He stopped talking and went back to using all his weapons against me. I had taken as much as I could, and I wanted to give him something in return. I grabbed at him, pulling him up my body until we were again face to face. His kiss tasted like me, his lips hot with my wet pussy. It was amazing.

"Me too, Blake. Me too."

I rolled him on to his back and straddled him quickly.

I ran my hands over his chest, feeling every inch of tight muscle and the light smattering of hair that covered his chest. I ran my thumbs over his tight little nipples, smirking at the hitch it caused in his breath. I leaned down and kissed his chest, smelling him, tasting him with my tongue. Licking tiny flicks over his nipple, I grabbed it lightly with my teeth, and he put a hand to my head. I went about torturing his nipples a little longer, letting his moans make me even hotter. His flat stomach beckoned me, and I let myself slide down his body. Kissing his navel, I felt his hard cock resting right between my tits. I let it drag over my soft skin, feeling it pulse and shake at the contact. It jerked forward, trying to get my attention. I smiled up at him, his eyes glassy and fuzzy with need. Keeping his gaze on me, I let my tongue fall gently out of my mouth and let the smallest lick move across the head.

I wrapped my lips around him, taking the soft, velvety head

between my wet lips. His gasp shot straight to my pussy, sending heat through me. I sucked him gently, until his eyes finally closed, his head digging back into the pillow. Slowly I licked my way down the under side of his cock, flicking and gently sucking the tender sensitive ridge. Licking my way back up, I wrapped my mouth around him again and let his cock sink deep, deeper into my throat.

"Oh God, Daisy. Please, let me fuck you."

I let the vibration of my stifled giggle buzz against him, and he let out a sharp moan. I took him deeper still into my throat, and his fingers stroked my neck, wrapped through my hair. My insistent, persistent sucking was driving him mad. The beautiful cut of his hips rested beneath my hands, the trembling I felt now passed on to him. He didn't let me go on much longer. Moving me gently up, he kissed me so hard, I thought I would never catch my breath. Every time I thought he was finished with my mouth, he kissed me again. Tongues plunging, tracing, finding new places to go. I was above him, his cock resting mere inches from my dripping wet pussy.

"I love you, Daisy."

"I love you too, Blake."

His name was barely out of my mouth when I felt the thick tip of his cock settle between my waiting cunt lips. He eased me down onto him, slowly inching me closer and closer to his body. When he slipped to the hilt, I rested on his lap, unable to move. I thought my body was going to come apart. His hands wrapped around my hips, gently rocking me front and back. Finally, my mind returned and I slid up and down his cock, feeling the sweet, deep pull of him with every stroke. I couldn't look away from his eyes. His hands freed my hips and roamed my body, touching off electric shocks with each pass. I was so deliciously full; his cock stretching me open, hitting deeper with each thrust. He pulled me forward to devour my mouth with his sweet kisses, taking my mouth. My clit was rubbing against his body, and I swirled my hips around in a circle as he plunged into me.

I felt my body tightening, every muscle building with tension and pleasure. His thumbs rolled over my nipples, the tight flesh barely able to take much more. My body was shaking, and I felt my orgasm building in me, deep and powerful. Blake let his thumb drop lower, and I felt it stroke over my warm wet clit, and I exploded. My body cried out violently, gripping Blake's cock deep inside me, my whole body contracting around him. I filled the silence of the room with my voice, my body releasing the pleasure that had been building. I rode against him, letting my body rise and fall, as pleasure seemed to be coming in never ending waves. Blake's hands dug deep valleys into my hips, and I felt his body turn to stone underneath me, his cock growing inside me as he grunted out his own orgasm, just as mine was ending.

We collapsed together, finished, spent. I rolled off Blake, feeling my body succumb to exhaustion. I felt like I couldn't move even if I wanted to. Blake wrapped his arms around me, pulling me into the safety of his embrace.

"That was amazing, Daisy. Exactly what we needed."

"Absolutely. And, I promise, no more DVDs, toys, or whips for a long time."

Blake laughed and pulled me up into a kiss, before waggling his eyebrows at me.

"Well, let's not be rash, Daisy. Maybe we can keep the whip."

# DRIVE ME CRAZY

Delilah Devlin

Just a glimpse of him standing in profile, arms crossed over his well-developed chest and leaning his firm, round butt against the dispatch counter, was enough to shore up my weakening resolve. Dressed in faded blue jeans, a black, chest-hugging T-shirt, and a red Razorback ball cap turned backward on his dark shaggy hair, he was every woman's blue-collar fantasy. My mouth dried as I glanced down his tall, muscled frame. What woman in her right mind wouldn't want one night with all that ripped hotness?

And that's all it could be—one night. I'd waited until the last possible moment to make my move.

The midnight drive to the dispatch office had given me plenty of time to argue my way out of what had seemed like a good plan earlier when I'd realized that the planets had aligned to give me this one last chance to fulfill my long-standing fantasy.

There'd never been the right time. For the longest time, I was married. When my husband dumped me, Danny had been living with a woman with two kids and seemed to be heading down a straight road to marriage.

We'd flirted; he'd issued lazy invitations for dates or a quickie at the Motel 6 down the road. But I'd never detected even a hint of serious interest. If something was going to happen, I had to be the one to make a move. Today had been my last day at Henderson Transport. It was now or never.

All the reasons why I was crazy to consider it fell away as I ticked through them in my mind:

*He's too young. He'll be happy because I won't have any expectations*, I said to myself. *Well, none beyond a really good time.*

*I'm management and he's a driver.* Midnight had just ticked past, so not true anymore. We were both free agents. Both consenting adults. All he had to do was say yes.

"You'll never see him again," I muttered under my breath as I rubbed my cold hands together. "If he turns you down, you won't have to live with his smug smile."

I sucked in a deep fortifying breath, adjusted the neckline of the red Lycra top to show my breasts to their best advantage, and pushed through the glass door.

His head turned at the sound, and then he straightened away from the counter and dropped his arms. "You cuttin' my route, Angela?"

I gave him a crooked smile. "Think I'd do that and ask you to wait for me here in the middle of the night?"

His brows drew together, curiosity glinting in his gaze before it dropped to my boobs. I'd worn a bra that pretty much left everything sitting on a shelf. My nipples were outlined against the red, stretchy fabric of my top, the tips spiking because I'd given them a little tweak before I'd exited my car.

His frown deepened. "What's this all about, Angela?"

I cleared my throat and tried for a sultry look. "I think you know."

He cocked his head and looked me up and down again. Slowly. "You don't have to hijack a man's keys to get his attention, sweetheart."

I planted my hands on my generous hips. "Apparently, I do, because you sure as shit haven't followed through on any one of your invitations."

His lips twitched. "I thought you flirted like that with all the guys."

"You ever see me do it? Even once?"

His jaw tightened. Fatigue showed in the shadows under his eyes. Stubble clung to his craggy cheeks.

I felt a momentary twinge of guilt over the fact I was keeping him from his bed, but that was all I'd allow. He was young and hot as hell. If he needed sleep that damn bad, he could tell his latest squeeze to come around another time. Tonight, he was mine.

"My keys weren't in the lockbox. I know I left 'em there."

"You did indeed," I said nodding. Then I looked him up and down, making sure he hadn't mistaken my intent. "Fact is, I have an itch that needs scratchin' and I'm hopin' you'll help me out."

I tried to exude more confidence than I felt, but I lost my nerve on the return trip up his hard body. I paused and swallowed hard, then gave a little cough to loosen the knot lodging at the back of my throat. When I reached his mouth, he was grinning.

*Shit.*

"Angela, is there somethin' you want?"

*You, preferably naked and tied spread-eagle on a bed so you can't stop me nibbling every edible part of you.*

"Angela?"

"Is there something I want? Yeah, there is."

"Then just say it."

But I couldn't. I felt foolish enough. I reached into my purse and drew out his key ring. "Look, I'm sorry. I shouldn't have taken this so far."

"You made me wait half an hour, when I could have been home, showered and in bed. You know how long I've been out this time."

"I know. I arranged the schedule."

Still, he didn't take the keys.

I took a step toward him and had to tilt my head to maintain the lock on his gray gaze.

His hands settled on my waist. "You want somethin', sweetheart?" he repeated, his voice lowering to a sexy rumble.

I squeezed my eyes shut, prayed for courage and that the blush staining my cheeks would fade. "I want you," I said, then opened my eyes.

His grin widened. "Now, was that so hard?"

"Matter of fact it was."

He bent toward me, his gaze narrowing on my mouth, but I turned away my face. "Not here. Your rig."

His eyebrows shot up, and he pushed me gently back. "After you. You know where I'm docked, and you have a key. Let yourself inside and get comfortable. I'm hittin' the locker room for a quick shower. I smell like diesel." He turned on his heel, giving me another view of that backside I'd drooled over for months.

A moan slipped from my mouth, and I heard a chuckle as he pushed through the door and left me standing weak-kneed in his wake.

He let me wait a good twenty minutes before the door to his cab opened, and he climbed inside. The scent of plain soap swept into the cab that already smelled like him—musky male, diesel. But since he didn't smoke and didn't appear to collect his meals, it smelled pretty good for a trucker's rig. Light shone from the top of a tall post in the parking lot, illuminating the cab. Security cameras would record who entered the truck but I hoped wouldn't disclose what we were about to do inside the cab. Another reason I'd waited until tonight for this. Everyone would be blabbing.

I sat in the plush leather passenger seat and glanced away as he climbed up into the driver's seat.

"Change your mind?" he asked softly.

"No," I bit out, a little annoyed that he asked. I wanted him to take the initiative, not seek my approval every step of the way.

"Then why aren't you in the back?"

"Look, you don't have to feel obligated," I said, turning to meet his smoky gray gaze. "If you'd rather get some sleep…"

"I jerked off in the shower."

My jaw sagged just a little, then snapped closed. "Now, why are you tellin' me a thing like that?"

"Because I want you to know how much I want you. Thought I'd take some of the edge off before I came out here. I didn't want to leave you unsatisfied, darlin'."

I swallowed hard, eyeing the taut edge of his jaw, the glint of arousal in his eyes. Maybe it was just what I wanted to see, but I didn't back away when he reached for me.

He leaned toward me. His hands slid around my back, one gliding up to fist in my hair. He held my head still as he devoured my mouth, lips rubbing over mine, his tongue stroking in to mate with mine. He tasted like minty toothpaste. The hands pulling me from my seat were strong, his grip firm. I didn't hesitate to follow his lead as he helped me rise and straddle his lap.

My skirt rode up past my hips, and cool air hit my bare

cheeks, but I didn't care. With the steering wheel rubbing my back, I settled over him, gripping his shoulders, at last feeling the muscles I'd admired for so long flex beneath my wandering palms. I tested his hardness, scratched down the deep indent of his spine, raked his scalp with my nails.

He broke the kiss and pushed me away. Then he tucked his fingers under the top edge of my red shirt and pulled down the stretchy fabric until the neckline cupped the underside of my breasts.

"Interestin' bra," he drawled.

I glanced down. My nipples and most of my fleshy breasts were exposed, sitting on a shelf of lace and underwire. "I hoped you'd like it," I said, my voice creaking like a dry hinge.

Thumbs and forefingers plucked my nipples, pinching and twisting gently, then tugging with more insistence. My heartbeats quickened, and blood surged to the aching tips, engorging them.

I flattened my hands against the back of his head and pulled him toward one spiked tip. I groaned when his mouth latched onto it. He nibbled and licked, bit and rolled.

I ground down against his lap, against the ridge thickening inside his jeans. I rubbed forward and back, the coarse denim building frictional heat between my legs.

One of his hands dropped to my ass, and he moaned as his long fingers dug into the skin bared by my thong. "Get into the back."

Breathing hard, I stared down. His mouth was blurred and red. His cheeks sharp, expression feral. The hardness in his gaze could have cut diamonds, and again, I didn't hesitate, no matter that my ass was in his face when I climbed between the seats to the sleeping berth.

The bed was mussed, the sheets wadded at one end. I lay

down on my side and scooted toward the back, waiting until he was clear of the seats and stretching out beside me.

Only his legs were too long and he lay at a diagonal, crowding my knees. I slid a thigh between his legs and climbed over his body.

When I sat atop his hips, he smoothed his palms up my torso, rolling up the shirt. When that flew over the seats, he reached around me and expertly opened the clasp of my bra. Without the underwire, I worried that my heavy breasts would sag too much, but he hefted them in his palms and his breaths deepened.

"I've wanted to suck on these forever."

I gave a short, strangled laugh. "I wouldn't have said no."

"Then why'd you wait so long?"

"Why didn't you make the first move? Are you really that arrogant that you have to have a woman come to you?"

"I didn't think you'd say yes."

"Really?"

He grunted, the sandpaper pads of his thumbs continuing to rasp over my nipples. "You're pretty. Smart too. And you have every man drivin' sniffin' after you."

"But you're handsome. I bet you don't get many no's from women."

He arched a brow.

"Okay, so not handsome like a movie star. But you're rugged and built like a god. I didn't think you'd want me. I'm too old for you."

"There's only eleven years between us."

I raised my brows. "How do you know that?"

"I ate your birthday cake and counted the candles."

When he pinched my nipples, I tensed, my eyelids dipping. "I guess eleven years doesn't really matter," I gasped, "when all we're doin' is screwin' around."

He pinched harder, then holding my gaze he came up on his elbows and rooted at one of my breasts, sucking the tip, and more, into his mouth. His moan was deep and gravelly. I felt it all the way to my toes.

My other breast tingled, dimples popping up around the areola and the tip sprung. I cupped it with my palm to ease the ache, but he pulled away my hand and shook his head, wagging my breast right along.

I gave a strangled laugh. "So not sexy."

He released my breast. "Got any complaints about my technique?"

"Maybe about your pacing." I ground against his erection. "You're killin' me here."

"Get your clothes off," he growled.

"You first."

"No way. I'm the guy. I get off on watchin'."

I swallowed hard, but I'd asked for this. Wanted for him to take charge, and he had with a vengeance if that hard-eyed look was any indication.

I slid down beside him and rolled to my back, then awkwardly tugged off my shoes, tossing them between the seats in front of us, then shimmied out of my skirt, being careful not to lose the scrap of lace shielding my sex from his hungry gaze.

Danny slid a finger under the lacy band at my hip, pulled it, and let it go to snap against my skin.

"Not nice."

"I didn't tell you to stop."

"You gonna order me around all night?"

"I think so," he murmured. "Seein' as how it turns you on." He traced a finger down the lace, right between my folds. He couldn't miss the moisture soaking through the satin.

When he popped his finger in his mouth for a taste, I pushed my panties down the rest of the way and then waited as he looked me over.

Danny traced down the edges of my nude outer lips. "Did you do that for me?"

I shook my head. "I prefer it."

"Spread 'em open for me."

I reached down and opened my lips and held them that way while he fingered the thin inner labia and pushed a long thick digit inside me.

My pussy clenched around him, then released. Then squeezed again. A trickle of moisture greeted his invasion, and he quickly pulled out and sat up in the small, cramped space beside me to tug his shirt over his head. He unbuttoned his jeans and pushed them past his hips. Just far enough to free his cock, which sprang free, lifting toward the ceiling of the cab.

I didn't wait for him to tell me what he wanted, he was too tight, too quiet, his breaths coming fast. I climbed over his knees and curled down to take him in my mouth. His fingers combed through my hair, then framed my face.

I bobbed down, my lips suctioning, latching around his crown to suckle hard, my tongue swirling over and over his soft, sleek head. I found the slit, teased it with the point of my tongue, then swirled again, sinking down his cock to take more of his length, caressing the sides of his thick shaft with my long, slippery glides.

His hand fisted in my hair and pulled me off. "Thought this was supposed to be your fantasy."

"Think I haven't thought about doing this? What it would feel like? How thick, how long it would be? I'm just gettin' acquainted."

"Damn. Come on up here."

I started to crawl up his body, sliding my chest over his belly, but he shook his head. "No, sit that bare-nekkid pussy over my mouth."

I pressed my lips together to keep the laughter trapped.

"Not cool enough?" he gritted out.

"It sounded sort of cheesy."

"Didn't I say it with enough snarl?"

"Just the right snarl if you were The King."

"Who?"

"Never mind," I muttered. *Baby.*

"I mean it. You got close and personal with me, turnabout is fair play. Bring it on up here, girl."

"I'm not a girl," I said, pushing out my lower lip.

He rolled his eyes. "Will you stop with the age thing? I want that pussy on my mouth."

The way he said it, his jaw tightening like he'd turn me over his knee if I didn't move fast enough, had me inching my way up until I squatted over his face, reaching up to curl my fingers over the edges of an overhead cabinet for balance.

Fingers parted me. He inhaled and gripped my ass in both hands and moved me slightly until my pussy made contact with his mouth. His lips latched onto me, sucking one side then the other, releasing me with moist pops that had me blowing out breaths in short, hard streams through pursed lips because it felt so damn good, so foreign. Like a dream come true because I'd imagined what it might be like and now it was happening.

Danny Echo was eating me out.

He gave long soothing strokes of his tongue and short ones that flickered over my soft wet edges. Then he hardened the point to flutter at my clit.

I couldn't hold still and began to rock in short glides, guided by his hands as I moved forward and back. I gave a moan when he rubbed his tongue harder over the swollen knot, burgeoning at the top of my folds and held still while he laved it over and over again.

"God, Danny, that's good."

"Like it?"

"Oh, yeah."

He gave my sex a loud smacking kiss, slapped my ass, and pushed me down his body.

I heard a tear, the slick snap of latex, and then he rolled, fitting me under him and thrusting his arms beneath my knees to lift my ass. "Put me inside you."

Both hands gripped his shaft, and he rocked forward. I aimed him right at my entrance, felt the nudge of his broad, round cap, and let go, bracing a hand against the wall and clutching the notch of his hip with the other as he entered me.

He was large. Perfect. Pushing gently upward, crowding through wet, swollen tissue that hadn't felt the stretch of a cock in good long time. Air hissed between my teeth, and I turned away my face.

"No," he said softly. "You wanted this. You have to watch." He reached and hit a light switch. The overhead glared down, exposing us both to the harsh, bright light.

I covered my breasts but couldn't help looking down to where our bodies joined. He pulsed inward, halted, and then pulled out. His shaft glistened with my juices. He slid his fingers around the base of his cock and squeezed. "Keep lookin' at me like that and I'll blow."

A smile tugged at the corners of my lips, and I knew I must have looked like the kitten licking up all the cream. I was the one who had his body so tight and hard that his belly shivered.

"Angela," he ground out. "Fuck." He released his grip, angled his cock just right, and slammed up my pussy.

My mouth opened and a long, thin groan joined the nasty

sounds echoing around the cab. Juicy slaps. Soft, masculine grunts. Short, metallic creaks. Coming faster as he pounded toward my core.

Release, when it came, roared through me. Toes curling, I snapped open my legs as wide as they could go, arched my back and sank my nails into his backside, trying to hold onto the moment because it was so damn perfect.

When my peak began to wane, he jerked, stroking in short, sharp bursts. Then he dug deeper at the last moment. His head fell back, his mouth opening around a loud, aching groan.

The sight of him, all primal male, chest and belly quivering, his cock still lodged deep inside me, was oh so gratifying.

At last, he gave a deep sigh and collapsed over me, my legs still wedged high, trapping his arms in the bend of my knee. I couldn't help it. I laughed.

His head jerked up. His gaze met mine, and his lips twitched. "Think I didn't do that on purpose?"

"Losin' circulation yet?"

He ducked and mashed his lips against mine, then backed up on his knees. His arms slid from under my legs, and I eased them down, stretching them on either side of his kneeling frame.

"So, I hear you're leavin'."

"Word gets around."

"Movin' out of town?"

I nodded. "To Prescott. I have another job. But how'd you know? I asked Cooter to keep it quiet."

His mouth widened. "Your new job. Dispatch for Ragland?"

I eyed him warily. "That's it. Just a good guess?"

He shook his head slowly, his smile never dimming.

Warmth centered in my chest. I ran my palms over his belly and scratched my fingernails down toward his groin. He came out of me, and I rolled the wet latex slowly down his length. "Lemme guess. You drive for them."

"Uh huh. Owner said this hot as hell woman from HT was hirin' on, and did I know you."

I pulled his cock hard, just to get his attention. "You couldn't have mentioned this earlier?"

He came over me, bracing his torso on his arms, a wicked glint in his gray eyes. "And have you spoil one fine-as-hell good-bye?"

# ONCE UPON A DINNER DATE

Saskia Walker

Samuel set the steaming platter of food down on the table with a flourish, intent on making an impression on his guest.

"This looks delicious," Cassie said, eyeing the food hungrily.

He was just about to move away when she reached out and grabbed his hand.

"Is this a proper date?" Her fingers meshed with his as she asked the question.

Samuel stared at her upturned face and for a moment he couldn't respond. The physical contact was too good, and the question was almost too direct—but it was exactly where he'd been planning to direct the conversation over the main course. Then she smiled that gorgeous smile of hers and the tension in his gut began to unravel.

"That was my intention," he replied. Acting on the sudden intimacy of the moment he drew her fingers to his lips, kissed them, then leaned down to kiss her mouth. Her soft lips parted under his, inviting him in, and when she wrapped her free hand around the back of his head and drew him closer still, physical need built quickly inside him, making him hard. How long he'd been waiting to do that, and now he knew she wanted it too.

"Don't let it get cold," she said as they drew apart, with mischief in her eyes.

*Not possible*, he thought as he took his seat at the table, opposite her. He wanted her too much, and being this close to her was driving him mad. She was a sensual, expressive woman with a warm, playful personality. That's what had drawn him to her, right from the moment she'd moved into the flat opposite his about six months before. He'd been attracted to her on sight, but given the age difference between them and her freshly divorced status, he didn't think he stood a chance. He was a research student in his mid-twenties. She was an advertising executive in her early thirties. Why in the hell would she give him the time of day? But she had, and now here they were.

"So, how long have you wanted to ask me on this date?" she asked as he dished the food from the platter onto her plate.

"Since you moved in." He smiled.

Her eyes flashed. "And there was me thinking it was Kyle you were interested in."

Samuel lifted one shoulder. "Hey, he's a good little gaming adversary."

It was true, but it wasn't the whole story. Six months ago he'd started chatting with her and her seven-year-old over the mailboxes each morning. Then he'd endeavored to help her out with her garbage on a Monday. She was grateful, and she chatted amiably. Before long he'd invited Kyle over for computer game time, and Cassie had come along to cheer them on. The three of them began to visit the nearby park together, and they enjoyed long conversations about life while watching over Kyle at play.

Slowly but surely Samuel's fascination with her had grown, until the nights grew restless and he knew he would have to take a chance and make a move.

When the weekend his flatmate was away coincided with the weekend that Kyle went to stay with his dad, Samuel took the chance to issue a casual invitation. Cassie had beamed, quickly affirming her intention to come over bearing wine and after-dinner mints. Now here she was in his tiny kitchenette, looking like the most sophisticated date a man could possibly wish for. When she'd walked in earlier that evening he'd nearly dropped the pan he'd been holding. The dress she wore was simple but elegant, with a low scooped neckline and a hemline that finished high on the thigh. Then there were the glossy shoes and stockings. When she'd sat down she had crossed her legs high on the thigh. He'd hardened immediately and had to turn away and pour himself a glass of water to help push the image from his mind.

"Sorry, that probably came across badly," he blurted, trying not to mess this up. "I didn't mean to imply I was spending time with Kyle to get to you."

"Don't worry, I didn't think that." She sipped her wine, then skewered a piece of Thai spiced chicken with her fork and took it to her mouth. She closed her eyes appreciatively as she ate the offering, savoring each and every morsel.

That wasn't helping him form sensible statements. He was having a hard time expressing himself, and this was important. He had to show her he was serious, and he had to know if she would take him—a younger man—seriously. "I enjoy Kyle's company, he's a great lad, but I was hoping to get to know you better as well."

"You will." With her napkin she dabbed at her lips.

The promise in her words made him want to rush through the dinner, or abandon it.

Gesturing at her plate with her fork, her face filled with something akin to orgasmic pleasure. "Mmm, I love Thai food."

"So I see." It seemed like the understatement of the century. It was a huge compliment to his cooking, but her expression wasn't helping Samuel to concentrate. And, if he wasn't mistaken, he could see her nipples outlined through the fabric of her dress. He'd never be able to smell lemongrass again without remembering the way she looked that night.

"Tell me, why didn't you ask me out earlier?"

Samuel stared across at her, his fork frozen midway between his plate and his mouth. "I wasn't sure you'd take me seriously, so I waited."

She nodded, looking deep into his eyes. "I was cautious with you at first, because I had to be sure I wasn't on the rebound. My husband left me for a younger woman, I wanted to be sure I was here for the right reasons."

That's what he'd surmised, and now he knew that she'd been anticipating this too, biding her time.

"As time went by," she continued, "I was sure. I'm not on the rebound. I've been hoping you'd ask me over."

He wanted to lift her into his arms and cart her off to the bedroom to celebrate.

As if she knew what he was thinking, she gave him a mischievous smile. "I'm not embarrassing you, am I?" she asked, as he tried to casually shift his food around on his plate. A sultry, suggestive look took up residence on her face and her lips glistened.

How was a man supposed to think about food when she was given him such an obvious green light? The woman he'd dreamed of getting close to for the past several weeks was practically stating they were going to have sex. "I appreciate your directness."

Samuel put his fork aside. He didn't want to eat. He wanted to bask in her presence.

"And I appreciate your cooking, among other things," she responded, and chuckled. The sound was earthly and sensuous, like everything about her.

"I'm flattered." He truly was. She ate the food as if it was heavenly, as if it was the best meal she ever had and she was with the man she wanted to be with. Did she know how that was affecting him? Samuel had his suspicions. There was a playful look in her eyes, and she seemed to be assessing him in some way. That made his temperature rise.

"This is why they always put me on the advertising accounts for food products, at work," she explained. "It's the flavors, they set my imagination on fire." Her gaze drifted over him.

The conversation was making his blood head south, but he wasn't complaining. "I can see the sense in that," he murmured.

"I'll let you in on a secret." She leaned forward, conspiratorially. "I think my taste buds are one of my most powerful erogenous zones."

There was absolutely no mistaking the naughty look in her eyes. Lifting his eyebrows, he said, "Oh, is that the case?"

"Uh huh. When it's a meal I really like, and I love spicy food, it really turns me on."

Samuel stared across at her as the implications slid fully into place. His inquisitive mind began to delve deeper, wondering to what extent that arousal manifested. Did she get wet? Did she want full-on sex as a result of it? The questions evaporated when Cassie held his gaze and reached for her fork, lifting another mouthful of Thai green curry. He watched as her glossy lips moved appreciatively while she ate the food. Another long *mmm* soon followed. He noticed then how she moved against the chair she was sitting on—it was a very real physical response.

His erection built when he wondered what it would be like to have her sit on his lap while she ate—what it would be like to feed her himself.

"My ex-husband hated it," she added. "It's a wonder we lasted nine years together." She chuckled again.

"Seriously?" Samuel was relieved that there didn't seem to be any regrets about the ex, and no impending reunion, a possibility that had entered his thoughts when he first thought about asking her over for a meal. The irony was that while he'd been cooking, he'd persistently reminded himself not to ask awkward questions about her divorce. All thought of that subject had evaporated when this absolute goddess had appeared and sat down at the kitchen table with him, as if dining out with a younger man while discussing erogenous zones was an everyday occurrence.

Her eyes twinkled. "When a meal is delicious as this, it's like really good foreplay for me."

Samuel ached for her. "I have to admit, the way you're enjoying the food is doing bad, bad things to me."

She dipped her finger against the corner of her mouth, wiping away an errant drop of sauce. "I noticed you've stopped eating."

When she licked that finger, he had to lean back in his chair. His cock was solid beneath the zip of his jeans, and all he could think about was sex. "I'm enjoying your meal way too much to worry about my own."

She nodded, as if pleased.

"I'm curious about how deeply it affects you," he added. *Was that pushing it too far?*

She didn't seem fazed by the comment, in fact she smiled. "Are you asking in your capacity as a biology research student, or something more personal?" She paused to sip her wine, which only seemed to emphasize the significance of what she was saying. "Don't be shy, Samuel. I'm a good nine or ten years older than you. We're both adults and we're attracted to each other. I was well aware that you didn't invite me over here just to feed me."

He exhaled, shaking his head in disbelief. He wasn't used to women being so generous and direct. He grinned. "Eight years, you're eight years older than me."

"I won't ask how you know that."

"I asked our landlady."

That amused her. "You have been doing your research."

He nodded. "Oh yes indeed. I only wish I was writing my doctoral thesis on you and your erogenous taste buds."

Her head dropped back as she chuckled. "Now that would be some fun research, wouldn't it?"

"I think so."

"What do you think it would entail, in your expert opinion as the biology grad student?" Her fingers trailed over the shoulder strap on her dress.

"Evidence," he stated. "Physical evidence."

"Well, in that case you better come over here and check me out for...evidence...don't you think?" She pushed her plate aside as she spoke, and then she eased her chair back from the table, wedging it against the cooker behind her.

Samuel couldn't believe his luck. She was inviting him to touch her, right here, right now.

Cassie watched Samuel as he stood, the pulse in her groin thudding wildly. He was an attractive young man, and he'd been keen from the outset. Caution had hampered this moment, but it had to happen. He'd won her over with his intense personality, green eyes, and rugged bone structure. Not to mention how fit he was—leanly muscled and tall, with the suggestion of vitality in his every move.

"I am so glad I made Thai food," he commented as he dropped to his knees before her, one hand resting on her knee. "This is like a dream come true."

"I think so too." She covered his hand with her own then swung her legs apart. "I want you, Samuel. I've been thinking about this, a lot."

"Me too." His gaze dropped. Tracing his fingers over the tops of her stockings, he sighed aloud. "You're beautiful."

"And you're supposed to be doing your research." Cassie was desperate to be touched, and if he didn't do it soon she would have to take matters into her own hands.

Shuffling her skirt up, she exposed her panties. She knew they'd be wet, and when she glanced down she could see a visible damp patch that followed the niche of her pussy.

Samuel swore low under his breath.

"Is that what you'd consider evidence?" she asked.

Sensible young man that he was, he thought about his response carefully before stating it aloud. It was one of the things that had tickled her about him. He was quietly ambitious, a risk taker, but he thought each comment out carefully before he took that risk.

"I need something more substantial," he eventually replied. Humor flitted across his expression.

"In that case I think you'd better investigate more closely, don't you?"

He nodded, and his eyes seemed to darken, his intensity growing by the moment. Cassie pursed her lips, her blood rushing as she waited for him to make contact.

He moved between her open thighs, then ran one finger down the side of her G-string—tantalizing her skin along the seam between her pussy and her thigh—before easing his finger under the fabric and homing straight in on her slit.

There was a slight tremor in his hand as he ran the back of one knuckle down the seam of her pussy, making brief but delicious contact with her clit. When she hummed her approval, he repeated the action. She leaned in and kissed his mouth, hands tight on his shoulders as she did so. He returned her kiss, their tongues thrashing as they hungrily explored each other's mouths. She could taste him too, and she wanted him.

Her open thighs wrapped more readily around his slim hips. The action enabled his finger to move lower, and within moments he had her panties pulled to one side and his finger had eased inside her.

"Oh yes, that's really good," she blurted when the hard digit slid inside her. She clutched it eagerly, and her upper body rested back against the chair. She pivoted on her hips, moving against his finger, her shoulders leaning against the knobs of the cooker at her back.

"Eat something," he whispered, nodding over at the table.

Cassie dipped her finger along the edge of her plate, then took it to her mouth and sucked the spicy sauce from it, watching him as she did so. The spices ran along her taste buds once again, making them tingle and spark. Her entire skin kindled, and her nipples chaffed against her dress. Her core clenched rhythmically, and the hard length of his fingers in there felt even better than before. "Oh, you're good!"

"I'll have you know I take my research very seriously." He got the comment out then groaned and peered down at her pussy as it clutched at him. "You're amazing," he added.

Cassie rocked her hips, riding his fingers. What she really wanted was his cock, and she could tell by looking at him that he would be ready and willing. "Didn't you say you had dessert?"

"Yes, tropical fruit marinated in amaretto."

She purred aloud and gyrated, getting hornier by the moment.

"Why don't you feed it to me while you're inside me...?"

She let that suggestion hang between them.

A moment later, understanding lit his expression. He removed his fingers, reached over to the fridge and pulled out a large, covered dish. As he did so Cassie caught sight of the bulge in his jeans. There was no doubting his state of readiness, and she quickly stripped her G-string off, ready—oh so ready—for more of everything.

Samuel clutched the bowl in one hand, the other closing over her bared pussy. There was a possessive look in his eyes. He squeezed her, as if he was testing her for ripeness. Then he lifted a piece of juicy mango from the bowl and held it out to her mouth.

She took the offering, licking his fingertips as she did so. He nodded, smiling. The texture and flavor was like a seductive dance on her tongue, the juicy fruit making her own juices flow all the more. "You make me feel greedy."

Samuel's eyes had grown hooded, and the smile that played around his mouth made him even more attractive. "You make me feel lucky."

He was clutching the bowl as if he was afraid of what he might do if he let go of it. It made her chuckle. "Put the bowl down on the table, and give me something harder."

She nodded down at his groin.

Samuel didn't seem to need to assess the risk of this potential action. No sooner than he had put the bowl aside, his fly was open and his cock was standing out to attention, long and hard and impressive in its girth.

Cassie rearranged herself on the chair, splaying her legs more thoroughly. She ran her fingers down her sex folds to hold them open, inviting him in.

Samuel stared at the offering. He shoved his hand in his jeans pocket and pulled out a condom. He quickly tore it open and donned the rubber.

Cassie's knees lifted around his hips as he pressed the blunt head of his cock to her opening, making her moan aloud. He hesitated, and she encouraged him on, tapping his bottom with one of her heels. "Samuel, I need you, badly. You've teased and taunted me with your delicious cooking. You've got me in a terrible state. You have to put me out of my misery and make love to me."

Samuel did not seem able to reply verbally, but his physical response was perfect. He grabbed her around the buttocks with both hands and gave her his length, inch by inch, before easing back then pushing in to the hilt.

Cassie expressed her gratitude audibly, her head going back as he stretched her open, filling her.

He kissed her throat while he found his rhythm, his hands clutching at her bottom over and over as he drove himself into her. In between damp kisses on her neck, he whispered her name and groaned.

"Oh, that's so good!" she cried.

"I've wanted you so badly." When he lifted his head to look at her she plucked a lychee from the nearby fruit bowl and put it into his mouth, then kissed him, scooping the fruit from his tongue to hers. The action sent him into overdrive, his hips thrusting against hers over and over.

When she bit into the succulent fruit and amaretto seeped onto her tongue she lifted her knees higher, angling his cock inside her. Her chair creaked and the front feet lifted, and she was grateful it was wedged against the cooker.

"Oh yes," she cried, when his cock thrust up against the front wall of her sex and hit against her center. "Promise me next time we do this we'll eat the whole meal this way."

Samuel stopped moving, and he cupped her jaw tightly in one hand as he looked deep into her eyes, forbidding her to look away. "Only if you promise me there will be many next times."

Her emotions soared, her body strung out on the ecstasy of the moment, his words and actions making a deep impression on her, just as he obviously intended. Unbidden tears welled in her eyes. For a while there she'd thought she would never feel like this, never want anyone this much ever again. Then Samuel had melted that away. She nodded, and clutched at him tighter still. "I promise."

He moved his hand and splayed it over her mons, thumb rocking against her clit, and then thrust again. Hard. "I want to feed you everything."

"Oh god, yes!" That thumb stroking over her inflamed clit made her pant aloud. Rocking her hips from side to side she gripped his shoulders with both hands. She reached her plateau and an intense wave of pleasure swamped her groin. Hot juices ran from the place where they were joined, soaking her buttocks and the chair beneath her.

Samuel soon joined her, his hips rolling in to hers over and over as he hit home and shot his load. Before he withdrew, he reached for another lychee, popping it between her lips. She bit the fruit and chewed it, savoring its intense flavor. He wiped a trickle of juice from the corner of her mouth.

"Are you sure you should do that?" she asked. "You'll get me started again."

"That was my intention." His smile was wicked.

She couldn't resist teasing him back. "Sure you can hack it?"

"Oh yeah, I've been hard thinking about you every night since I first saw you, and I've got a lot of erections to work off."

Cassie gestured at the fruit bowl. "In that case I believe it's time to adjourn to your bed. You grab the fruit, I'll bring the wine."

Samuel grinned. "You got it."

As they stood, wobbly and laughing, she clutched him to her. "I like you Samuel, I like you a lot."

He cupped the back of her head and kissed her deeply. "I like you too, a lot. In fact I think I fell in love with you weeks ago. Does that worry you...?"

There was a challenge in his eyes. He really was a very intense sort of man, and that set her alight. "Not any more." She ran her fingers along his jaw, sighing happily. "One thing I ought to say, though," she added.

A concerned look flitted across his eyes.

"You must let me take my turn cooking....otherwise you won't get to know which meal turns me on most of all."

The concerned look disappeared and he grinned. "It just gets better and better."

She trailed her finger along his jaw. "When I like something this much I always come back for more."

# HE TENDS TO ME

Justine Elyot

He hates it when I'm ill.

He hides it well, replenishing magazines and tissues, haunting the pharmacy, inventing new recipes for hot toddies, but I know that this evidence of disorder in his world disturbs his equilibrium. Because Matthew's world must be, above all things, perfectly ordered.

My strep throat was not on the agenda for this month, and therefore all is awry and out of kilter. It's worse for me, of course. I had to cancel a series of concerts, for a start. But Matthew has lost his control of the universe, which usually drives him to demonstrate his mastery of life a little closer to home. At my sickbed.

I am accustomed to Matthew's bedside manner, so when I arrived home on a rainy wintry night with unusually heightened color in my cheeks and greeted him with a croak, I knew what was coming.

He leapt up from his writing desk and put a cool palm to my

forehead, shaking his head and muttering.

"You're feverish," he diagnosed. "Get to bed. Now."

Usually these words are enough to gladden my perverted heart, but when he says them without sexual intent they are even more powerful.

I was happy to obey, crawling between the covers and shivering there until he appeared at my side with a thermometer—not the one we sometimes use in doctor and patient role plays, thank goodness—and a glass of hot water with honey, lemon, and a nip of brandy.

"What have you been doing to yourself?" he asked sternly. He always accuses me in this manner when I fall ill, as if I have somehow invited the infection in.

"Nothing!" I defended myself. "Germs don't care what you do. If they're out to get you, they will."

"Are you sure you weren't flirting with them?" he said, his severity containing a more playful note.

He made me open my mouth and stuck the thermometer beneath my tongue, muting me for the half-minute it took to get a reading.

"Because if I thought you were giving those streptococci the come-hither, Loveday, I would be most displeased. And you know what happens when I'm displeased, don't you?"

I nodded, wanting to bite my lip but finding the gesture impeded by the slim glass tube resting upon it. I knew what happened when Matthew was displeased. But it wasn't anything he could do to a person with strep throat, so I considered my bottom safe for the moment.

He whipped out the thermometer and read it with a frown.

"I think you're officially ill," he said. "We'll have to add my current displeasure to your account. I'm going to give you three days, Loveday. For every day beyond that that you are coughing or sniffing or spending the most part asleep, there will be a penalty."

"That's not fair," I said, my voice coming out in the wrong register.

He tutted and took my burning hands, stroking them.

"When have I ever been fair?"

It was a good point.

"So you need to make sure you get well as soon as possible, won't you?" he whispered. "No getting out of bed without permission. No trying to talk when your voice isn't ready. No disobeying Dr. Rossington's orders."

"No fun," I mouthed with a pout, and he gave my hands a light tap of reproof.

"Not until you're better. Now get some sleep."

Swimming in and out of consciousness, I sometimes heard him on the phone, canceling engagements and giving explanations of my absence.

He brought cool cloths for my forehead and antiseptic lozenges for my throat. He was as efficient a nurse as anyone could wish for. Perhaps a little too efficient.

When I staggered to the bathroom without waiting to ask his permission, it was made clear to me that I had transgressed. He waited outside the door for me and, on my exit, he took me by the shoulders and steered me back to the bed.

"Since you can't be trusted to do as you're told," he said, "perhaps I need to tie you to the bed. Hmm? Should I?"

"No," I whispered. "I'll ask next time."

"You've got your phone. If I'm in another room, just send me a message."

"I will."

I collapsed into the blankets again and let them take me into their too-hot embrace.

For two days I languished, but on day three, I began to rally. My voice was still more like that of a pubescent boy than a professional soprano, and my head still felt stuffed with wadding, but my spirits made a brisk reentry, and so did my libido.

I picked up the mobile phone and began to text. I knew that Matthew was composing in the other room, but he'd had two uninterrupted days with his muse. Surely she could spare him for a little while.

"I need a doctor," I wrote, and pressed Send.

He appeared in the doorway in a matter of seconds, his face pale.

"Are you alright, Loveday? Why do you need a doctor? Are you feeling worse?"

Feeling slightly guilty, I shook my head.

"I meant you," I warbled. "I need Dr. Rossington."

The color returned to his cheeks, and he raised a disapproving eyebrow.

"You mean you just worried me on a whim?"

"I didn't mean to. I just felt the urgent need for some... medical attention." I tried to look sexy, which wasn't easy in an old-lady nightgown and socks, but it seemed to work because he came all the way into the room and stationed himself at the foot of the bed, arms folded, brow creased in that thrilling way I love so much.

"Medical attention? Well, I think I can provide that. Take off your nightgown."

I pulled the sagging cotton over my head and peeled off the socks too, since he'd never expressed a kink for them, while he left the room.

When he came back, he was carrying a basin of soapy water and a sponge.

"Let's start with a bed bath, shall we?"

He pulled out the rubber sheet from underneath the bed and made me lie flat on it, its cold smooth texture immediately transporting me back to the other occasions it had been in use, bringing my reawakened sex drive to even more vivid life.

I curled my toes and clenched my vaginal muscles, enjoying the sight of him rolling up his shirtsleeves before he reached for the sponge.

He held it above me and I jolted, emitting a soundless squeal, as cold water dripped on to my naked breasts.

"Don't move," he ordered. "Or I'll tie you down. Keep perfectly still."

It was almost impossible not to squirm or shield my upper body as each drop fell delicately and with deadly impact onto my stiffening nipples or goosepimpling belly. I balled my hands into fists and tried to hold my breath—one thing I'm very good at—until he relented, poured some warmer water into the basin from a jug and loaded the sponge with soothing suds.

They glided over my body, leaving their trail of foam, as Matthew washed me from my neck downward, moving the sponge with loving expertise between and beneath my breasts, round and round the elliptical mound of my abdomen and then onward.

"Let's get you nice and clean," he said, under his breath as if talking to himself. "And ready. Ready for your treatment."

My pussy hardly needed the sponge to dampen it; his words and his calm, authoritative manner had already set the juices flowing. But he washed between my thighs diligently, moving the sponge closer and closer until it parted my lower lips, dabbing the foam on and around my clit, making it sting just a little bit.

I sucked in air and jiggled my hips.

"Oh dear. You moved. Legs wider, please, I think we'll need a little more attention to this area."

I didn't want more soap on my clit, but I did as I was told, somehow making it through the extra cruel ablutions, though I don't think I managed to keep as still as he required me to.

"I hope I don't need to tell you," he said, picking up a razor and beginning to scrape away the three-day growth of hair from my genital area, "that you are forbidden to strain your voice. Any crying out or making a sound will be punished."

I cursed my bedridden horniness. I might have known Matthew would be a terrible doctor. But despite my apprehension, my stomach was curling over and over inside, tautening into a knot of sheer lustful excitement.

"Right," he said briskly, discarding the razor. "On to your stomach."

This was always a dangerous position to be in if you were in Matthew's vicinity, but I rolled over and presented him with my rear view. The warm soapy water spilled deliciously from my shoulder blades down into the hollow of my back, pooling in the crease of my buttocks. Matthew swabbed away at the cheeks he made such endless use of, wiping them clean and finishing with a deep cleansing sweep of the crack between.

I heard the sponge splash back into the basin and then I blanched as Matthew's fingers kept my bum cheeks spread.

"Now, about that fever," he murmured. "We need to make sure your temperature's down before we go any further."

I repressed a whimper. A lubricated finger circled my quivering asshole, preparing it for the slow slide of the cold glass thermometer.

"Most patients would have their temperatures taken with a digital ear thermometer," explained Matthew, pushing it further in, inch by inch, and rotating it slowly inside my bum. "But not you. You're different, Loveday. You need special treatment. It says so on your notes."

"Does it?" I whispered.

"Yes, it does." He held the thermometer fully in, his thumb and finger resting between my cheeks. "It says, 'Patient needs firm handling at all times. Facilitate her swift recovery with frequent rectal examinations and strict discipline.' The consultant seems very sure that this is what you need."

"Stupid consultant," I whispered, just loud enough to be audible.

"What was that?" Matthew withdrew the thermometer in one swift stroke, leaving my sphincter muscles trembling at the unexpected vacation. "I see from my thermometer that you are not too ill for a spanking, young lady. Disrespecting the consultant certainly merits one. In fact, I think he should be here to witness it...but I think he's on another call. Never mind. You can imagine him here, and I'll write up a report on your punishment for the notes, just so he knows."

I twisted my ankles and wrists, antsy and tense on my rubber sheet. I both dreaded and longed for the promised spanking, and I worked on my readiness for the first stroke, but instead he picked up the sponge again and wrung it out on my bottom so that the water flowed over the cheeks and down my hips, puddling on the sheet.

When his hand fell, I nearly jumped up to my knees. I thought I knew the exact form and feel and weight and shape of his open palm, but this felt quite different, and it stung substantially more than I remembered.

"Ha ha," he chuckled delightedly. "That's how it feels on a wet bottom. I've heard it's more painful. So it's true."

He continued to smack at my dripping bottom until it was dry—a long and intensive process throughout which it was impossible not to wriggle and kick and make pathetic squeaking noises.

"There," he said, rubbing the site of his evildoing. "A red, sore bottom is very good at aiding recovery for minxes like you. I think we'll repeat that prescription thrice daily."

"Thrice?" I moaned. "But it hurts."

"The best medicines are hard to swallow," lectured Matthew. "Speaking of which...but no. I can't be sure the infection has cleared up yet. We'll have to find another way of administering the dose."

"The dose?" I wanted to laugh. That was one way of putting it. If I panted, "Dose me up, doctor," in the throes of orgasm, would that work for him?

"The medicine you need," he whispered, bending down to my ear. "The medicine you're going to get."

"Can I ask for a second opinion? Ouch!"

My bottom quivered in the aftermath of the unexpected smack. I supposed that was a no.

He bobbed down under the bed again, looking for more devilish implements.

"It's an unorthodox treatment," he said, coming back up. "I'm writing up my findings for the medical journals. It's proving very effective, but it can be a little difficult to administer if the patients are too mobile. So..."

He applied a leather cuff to my left wrist, chaining me to the outer post of the headboard.

"...I think restraints are in order...but it's nothing to worry about...."

He repeated the process with my right wrist.

"It's all perfectly safe. Trust me. I'm a doctor. Now, get up on your knees and spread them."

Promptly I obeyed, slipping about on the wet rubber sheet until I was positioned for optimum obscene display.

"If you make a sound," he cautioned, "the treatment will be

ineffective and I will have to use something stronger on that sore bottom of yours. So complete silence for this, understand?"

I nodded, full of joyful dread.

"It's called orgasm therapy," he told me. A smooth bulb-shaped presence made itself felt at my cunt. "Come-vales-cence."

"Oh, that's terrible," I groaned, and then I squeaked as the bulbous head of the vibrator was shoved unceremoniously forward, breaking through yielding flesh and lodging inside.

"I said silence! That's five strokes of the strap for you, later."

I held my breath and concentrated on the easy passage of the silicone intruder up to its full length, where it rested for a while before beginning to buzz gently.

Matthew's fingers, now sheathed in surgical gloves, manipulated my clitoris, bringing it to its swollen point of no return, making me gasp silently and strain against my bonds. His exact and precise knowledge of my most intimate places frightened me sometimes. It was as if he had a book stored in his head called *How to Touch Loveday*, every word of which he had memorized. Heat rushed to the spot, and the slow vibrations inside me brought me to a first rapid climax. Mixed with the intensity was an edge of panic as I wondered if orgasmic silence was possible. Why hadn't he gagged me? It would make things so much easier. Oh. That was why.

I bit my lip, pulled at my bonds, let the tremors build up and radiate through me, concentrating on feeling myself at the center of them rather than expressing them in my habitual broken yowls.

"You're coming, aren't you? That's good. Very good. Let it out. That's right. But we haven't finished yet."

He switched up the setting on the vibrator, placed a buzzer

on my clit, and moved his soaked gloved fingers up the crack of my bum to find the unoccupied hole. I wanted so badly to cry out when he began the loving, unhurried business of lubrication, but I held back, my thighs shuddering, cunt in turmoil, sore throat totally forgotten, while he circled and probed, circled and probed, over and over and over.

"I think this is where the dosage will be given," he pronounced.

A low sound would have escaped me, if my faulty throat hadn't provided salvation. My head was in thrall to my body, my instructions and resolutions on the verge of being forgotten. I had to remember to be quiet. I had to make sure the treatment worked.

His fingers spread my tight-furled asshole, preparing it thoroughly, examining its depth and width with scientific care.

"Yes," he said. He was struggling to stay calm, I could tell, and I was struggling not to come, wanting to save myself for the moment of possession.

Over the buzzing and the insistent roar of my blood in my ears, I heard the unbuckling of belts, the lowering of trousers, the removal of undergarments and then he was behind me, holding my flanks, nudging up against the vibrator at first then parting my cheeks.

"Take your medicine," he breathed, then his impossible width amazed me anew by edging through my anal defenses, gathering lube on the way.

I puffed and clenched my fists, trying not to resist, trying to wrap myself up in the dark comfort blanket of total submission, feeling and knowing myself to be his in every way. Penetrated in every orifice except the one I had to keep such stringent control of, I slid down inside myself, becoming a creature of sex and surrender, a helpless patient having to accept that my doctor knew better than me.

The dosage was strong and the side effects included some discomfort and a few pangs, but the best medicine has unpleasant features, so I accepted it willingly, pushing myself back to take his entire length, showing him my trust.

"That's good," he said, beginning a slow thrust, rubbing up against the vibrator in my other hole with each push forward.

I came again, my body defeated and dominated, and then once more before he granted me the vital injection. He used me hard, leaving finger marks on my hips and my bottom burning, but the exhaustion I felt on his withdrawal was oddly invigorating—it was no longer the exhaustion of sickness, but of healthy exertion.

While I lay on the damp rubber sheet, trying to remember what was supposed to be wrong with me, he kissed the length of my spine and then arose, disappearing for a moment.

When he came back, he patted me down with a towel before uncuffing me, helping me to my feet and removing the rubber sheeting.

"I think you need to go back to bed rest," he said, holding me close, his arms crossing my rib cage, "if we're going to continue this treatment."

I let myself lean back against him, boneless in the aftermath, while he kissed my neck and shoulders, and then I was tucked back into bed and my real temperature taken.

"It's well down," he said. "For some reason. I would have expected that kind of treatment to elevate it. But what do I know? I'm not a doctor."

"Hey," I croaked. "You aren't? So...what was that?"

His wickedest smile shone down on me.

"That was for your own good," he said. "Now I'm going to call your doctor and ask what he recommends for girls who are well enough to be taken vigorously up the ass yet who protest that they can't go back to work yet."

"No you aren't, you swine!"

"Yes I am. Or rather, no I'm not. Because I know what he'd say. I know what he'd write on his prescription form. Something painful involving your behind and my hand, I suspect. So you'd better get some rest while I work my strength up."

I pouted, but I felt blissfully, floatingly sleepy.

"Thank you," I yawned. "You might not be a doctor, but I think I'm cured."

He leaned over and kissed my forehead, his blue eyes earnest as he drew back.

"I'm very glad to hear it," he said. "Gladder than you know."

I know he hates it when I'm ill, but I don't think it's all about control and inconvenience. I think it's mostly about love.

# GUEST SERVICES

Angela Caperton

Joanna Danvers checked her watch again, the third time in the past hour. Maybe he had canceled late. Severe weather in the Northeast had caused more than one Suite Rewards guest to change their plans and their reservations.

Damn. Her heart constricted at the thought that Thomas Wolburn might not check in today. This was it; this was Joanna's last weekend at Suite Rewards Miami. On Wednesday, she'd pack her Focus with everything she could fit into it, leave her furniture to the mercy of movers, and head north to Atlanta and Suite Rewards' corporate headquarters. She'd done it. After six years of busting her ass, first as the concierge and then as manager of guest services at the busy Suite Rewards Executive Hotel Miami, she'd been promoted to regional manager. Yes, she'd be back to Miami, but she'd also be in Savannah, Jacksonville, Tampa, Mobile, Orlando, and several other southern locations—but most often in her office in Atlanta.

Thomas Wolburn would no longer be the steady fixation

of her lustful dreams. His clockwork stays at Suite Rewards Miami, three times a year for the past four years, had helped kill two vibrators in Joanna's nightstand. Part of her loved him, loved his smile, even after a six-hour delay in his flights, loved his wit and intelligence, plus he had an ass to make women drool. She knew he wasn't conventionally handsome—a faded scar from forehead to jaw dropped his left eyelid to near closing and his nose was crooked, but Joanna would have gladly sold her soul to have his minty-green eyes look at her lustfully, or to have him kiss her, his lips so generous she sometimes wondered if he patronized Botox clinics. She had fantasized many times about those full lips locked around her nipples or rubbing against her clit.

The job in Atlanta had been a fantasy too. She still chafed at the comment made at her interview by Les Grinion. "Joanna, you could have had this job a lot sooner if you'd had the nerve to take it."

Nerve to take it. Hadn't that been the story of her life? When had she ever just taken something? She never stepped outside her safety zone, never threw caution to the wind and just *took* something for herself.

Life just happened to her. She'd become a wife because Mark had asked and because she didn't think anyone else would. Five years later, divorced and up to her gills in debt, she took a desk clerk job at Suite Rewards because it had been the first thing she had been offered. She worked diligently and, when their concierge quit, she had been assigned to cover his desk until a replacement could be found. Joanna learned five months later they never posted the position. She'd been promoted, and no one had even bothered to tell her. Until she mentioned it tentatively, her title and pay hadn't changed.

Once she knew that she wasn't just a placeholder, she owned

the position. She charmed entertainment and restaurant contacts in South Beach, Little Havana, and other hot spots in Miami, made sure the hotel was on the lodging list for every appropriate event, maintained an aggressive local events calendar on the Suite Rewards website, and made sure guests were emailed important notices in advance. She developed inside sources, like the one who helped her get courtside seats to a Miami Heat playoff game for an important guest. She was good at her job, and she enjoyed it.

And she loved it every time Thomas Wolburn, on his periodic visits, joined her for a drink in the hotel bar after hours. It had become a ritual, even after she'd been promoted to Guest Services manager. She closed the restaurant at 1 A.M. and stayed there with him, behind the bar, pouring drinks for both of them. The first time had been an accident. Joanna had been filling in for one of the desk clerks when Tom came in at closing time, looking tired. After that, the post-midnight liaisons had become a delightful ritual between them.

Those quiet conversations over good bourbon had fueled Joanna's infatuation and her lust. She began to regard Tom's visits like paid vacations to Hollywood. He was certainly her favorite guest and, as strange as it seemed, her best friend.

He liked Josh Ritter's music, and he smoked cigars on very special occasions. He hated having his birthday the week before Christmas and on one overindulgent night, halfway into a bottle of Russell's Reserve, he told her about the accident that scarred him and almost killed his sister, how he'd been driving and arguing with her about which radio station to listen to.

That night, cotton-soft and warmly flush, she took his hand, thrilled at his skin against hers. She wanted to invite herself up to his room. She wanted to fuck him very, very much, but she choked on the words, her mind dizzy with possibilities, risk analysis, the probability of complete humiliation. She didn't have any condoms with her. Would he? No, no. No condoms, no go. Tomorrow. Yes, tomorrow, she'd bring a jumbo pack of Trojans and they'd fuck the night away. Yes, yes. She'd just wait, and tomorrow she'd offer him some exclusive hotel services.

Yes.

No. The next night, as Joanna lingered at the concierge desk, ostensibly checking guest requests, she watched Tom leave with a tall, svelte woman who could have been Miss Brazil 2010—long black hair, eyelashes to die for, dark eyes and full lips that must have graced at least one fashion magazine. If there hadn't been boxes under her desk, Joanna would have crawled under it.

The Trojans rescinded to the very back of her bottom desk drawer, under padded half-sized envelopes and behind a dog-eared copy of *Delta of Venus*.

When next Tom visited, she joined him for a drink, but she didn't even think about trying to seduce him. No, better to tackle him only in her fantasies, to tear his clothes off, suck his cock until he begged her to fuck him, then she would mercilessly ride him until she was good and ready to come. Maybe she'd let him come then. Maybe. Fuck the Brazilians.

After that, his visits had been pleasant, and her desire for him had remained undimmed and unfulfilled, but she had never again considered crossing the line between friendship and bare flesh. And now time was running out.

The nerve to take it. What did that mean? She glanced at the clock at the corner of her monitor screen. The nerve to take it. Nerve that didn't guarantee she'd get what she wanted, just that she'd had the courage to reach for it.

Yes, she'd need nerve if she was going to rip Les Grinion's job from under his tasseled shoes. The Atlanta office was a cutthroat place to work. She'd need smarts, timing, and nerve. It was one thing to plan, it was another to execute, and fear of failure was not an acceptable excuse. That was Les's unwitting gift to her— that kernel of realization, and she had every intention of making it his final condescension.

Just like the job, Tom Wolburn was something—someone— she wanted, and this would be the last time she could count on seeing him. She had to do this. She had to reach out, to bridge the distance between their clasped hands, to turn confidence and comfort into sex. She had to, even knowing he'd almost certainly reject her. That was Les's message. Executives took risks—sure, they weighed profit against loss and sometimes they guessed wrong, but those who succeeded *took risks*!

She had to put herself out there. Joanna knew if she left Miami without even trying to hook up with Tom, she'd not only regret it all her life, the regional manager's desk in Atlanta would be the terminal point in her career.

The warm tap of shoes on the marble foyer drew her out of her thoughts. Tom! There he was, the back of his suit jacket creased from hours of sitting, and he looked as if he'd shrunk a couple inches. The bolt of concern singed more than her heart. Recurrent guests passed through lives beyond her knowing, and she had seen more than one decline between visits, eroded by health or misfortune. No, he couldn't be one of those.

She waited patiently as he checked in, and before he turned away from front desk, she'd stepped into his path, her skirt standard uniform, her blouse sheer to show off the embroidered bustier under the black silk.

"Now there's a sight for sore eyes." He looked as though he meant his words as he took Joanna's arm, gripping it in friendly possession as he kissed first her check and then her lips, a warm but chaste kiss.

"And here I am—just for you," Joanna returned the kiss.

"I've learned over my years in Guest Services that the best way to find out what a customer wants is to ask directly." She pressed tight against Thomas, unconcerned about the desk clerk who mechanically finished processing Tom's reservation. "What do you want, sir?" she whispered against his ear.

She absorbed the stiffness of his body. The awkward words would come any second, the no's and stumbled, polite dismissals, the adjustment of the distance between them. Maybe he'd say he really liked her as a friend and that sex would ruin things. Maybe he'd confess to being married/engaged/seeing someone, or—she grinned against his shoulder—he'd tell her regretfully that he was gay. The rejection would come, but it would be all right. She'd taken the chance.

He pulled her closer, and she imagined his comfortable business mind melting and mixing into goo as her pussy pressed against his thigh, and...his cock stiffened.

"I want *you*," he whispered against her ear.

She blinked, her bones suddenly marble, her skin the thinnest sheet of breath that burst into hot sensation where his fingers held her against him. That was a yes—he'd said yes. That wasn't supposed to happen!

Could she unbury the condoms in less than 2.6 seconds, and what the hell did this mean in the grand scheme of her... scheme?

"Come with me," she breathed against his chin. She'd take him to her office, manage a moderately graceful excavation of the condoms, and then they'd fuck on her desk. All she had to do was toss the two copier paper boxes filled with her personal mementos to the floor and they'd have a wide plane to play upon. Maybe he'd bend her over the edge, fuck her mercilessly from behind. What if he slapped her ass?

Her pussy creamed.

"No," he exhaled, the quiet tone reaching the tenor of a growl. "I want my bed turned down. Personally."

She nodded, a bob of her head she doubted anyone would have seen. That was her job. Guest Services. Yep, turning down beds was right up her alley.

"Of course, sir," she purred.

"Naked."

The pulse of arousal that blasted her core nearly brought her to her knees—not that the vantage of her face level with his crotch would have been unwelcome, but she still wanted to keep some level of dignity.

"After you, sir," she said, her throat dry even as her cunt continued to slick.

He grinned, a lopsided expression that constricted her heart. He put his arm around her waist and walked to the elevator. Joanna glanced at the front desk. Martin, the college kid they'd hired that spring, was staring at her as if she were a three-headed alien.

All she could do was smile.

Tom's room was on the top floor. They had the elevator to themselves and, when the doors closed, their bodies merged. His mouth devoured her, tongue insistent, hot, demanding, tangling with hers, suppressing it, dominating it even as she grappled with him, losing herself in the sensations his kiss invoked. She felt the heat of his body in one long, glorious line of firm muscle and strength. His cock pressed hard into her thigh, and she could not wait to have it in her.

He pushed her against the back of the elevator, pulling up her skirt, greedy fingers stroking her thighs, finding her panties, and sliding beyond the thin lace to her soaked pussy.

He groaned, his kiss deepening further, and Joanna answered his arousal by gripping his ass, longing for the firm flesh to be free of his trousers. Boxers or briefs, what would it be?

The chime rang almost mute beneath their panting and groping, but when the doors opened, Joanna moaned against Tom's mouth, pushing him toward the gate, closer to fulfillment.

His fingers circled her clit.

The suction of the kiss broke as she pushed him, grinding her hips against his hand, gasping for air. He stepped back, their dance made of steps banned by Arthur Murray. His heel caught on the metal lip of the elevator as they stumbled back, balance completely lost until his thighs hit the back of the sofa in the elevator landing. Golden wallpaper with subtle fleur-de-lis appliqués rose to a ceiling dominated by a tasteful, frosted light fixture. Several other upholstered chairs, end tables, and two huge vases filled with fresh flowers furnished the little lobby.

He spun, a final effort to save both of them a tumble over the couch back. When Joanna's butt hit the top of the sofa she welcomed the full weight of him, the momentum of their fall pressing him harder into her. Her lips found his again, ravenous, drawing his flesh into her even as his fingertips stroked the folds of her pussy and slid easily into her. Electric bites of pleasure zapped her nerves, spreading heat and sensation through her. Her hips ground against his hand spastically, graceless, but honest and greedy.

Tom continued to press her against the back of the sofa, pulling her skirt up, her panties down. He took his hand from her clit long enough to pull her blouse free of the waistband of her skirt, reaching under it, under her lace bra to her breasts, cupping them as if he weighed them, testing her hard nipples, circling the tips until she panted. He pulled back just enough to turn her away from him, so that his cock bumped her butt. He pinned her, holding her still, and when he took his hands from her, she felt like a boiling pot with the fire suddenly turned off.

The crinkle and tear of plastic registered moments before his hands again found her skin, one stroking the curve of her ass, the other stroking up the crack of her pussy, teasing her, spreading her.

The stroke of his cock head along her pussy lips nearly shoved her over the edge. Coated in her juices, he pressed into her from behind, his cock thick, hard and gloriously filling. His exhalation bordered on a moan, and with his balls slapping her butt, he paused, buried deep.

Joanna drew a constricted breath that barely seemed real. She was doing it. She was getting fucked by Tom Wolburn. Another elevator might arrive at any moment, or someone might emerge from the hall into the lobby, but she was beyond caring.

His first few strokes were slow, testing, and amazingly smooth. She savored every inch, her nerves blooming beyond physical stimulation but into something so intense it seemed almost artificial, like some glorious drug that dulled mundane cares and magnified bliss. The beat increased rapidly, his cock splitting her, taking her, marking her, a precise pattern of stretching nerves and tearing lust that left her powerless to do anything other than brace her arms on the seat of the sofa and take it.

Her clit bumped and bumped against the edge of the sofa, adding another layer of pleasure and as orgasm rose in her, she squeezed her eyes shut and bit her lower lip against the scream so near to utterance.

Gold walls melted to crystal. Her ears rang with the scuff of the sofa as Tom's thrust pushed it into the coffee table. The shudder began at her knees and overwhelmed her body as the orgasm rocketed through her. Her locked elbows buckled, and her face met the back cushion of the couch.

She just knew her muffled scream could be heard down in the main lobby.

He pulled her back against him and gave three more hard, rapid pumps before he huffed, made a sound that resembled a gurgle, then folded over her, panting into her spine.

She couldn't move, didn't want to move. He kissed her back at the edge of her disheveled blouse, his hand reaching around her middle to hug her, a contented, but possessive hold that frosted the fading edges of her orgasm, sweet and rich.

He started to shake, then his chuckle cut through her fuzzy curiosity.

"Fuck."

She grinned into the cushion. "Accurate."

"No. I forgot my suitcase at the front desk." He pulled out of her, his softened cock leaving her suddenly hollow.

She stood up, her muscles protesting after her prolonged half-crunch. She turned, pulling her shirt and skirt down and watched him wrap the used condom in his handkerchief.

She pushed at her hair and grinned at him.

"No problem. Go on to your room. I'll bring your luggage up."

She stepped up to him and gave him a playful kiss. "And, of course, I'll see about that turn-down service."

He squeezed her waist and grinned. "Hurry."

And she did, riding back down to the lobby, her heart racing, the glow at her center far more than just the result of good sex. Maybe this was what nerve felt like, the illumination of possibility, the reward worth any risk. She found his suitcase at the desk, gave Martin a wink, and caught the elevator back up.

All the way to the top.

# MEMORIES FOR SALE

Andrea Dale

Bella knew this was a bad idea.

She'd known it when she'd turned her car off the highway and headed for the lake. She'd known it when she passed the "For Sale" sign at the end of wooded drive. She'd known it when she got out of the car and smelled the early autumn air, with its melancholy reminder that the seasons changed, that time moved on. That the past was lost.

She'd known it when she twisted the key in the lock and opened the front door.

The realtor hadn't bothered with a lock box. The open house tomorrow would bring a slew of interested buyers, and there would be a bidding war for the vacation home.

Bella had simply wanted to see the place one more time.

No, not *simply*. There was nothing simple about divorce. She and Ethan had agreed to sell the cabin prior to the final paperwork and split the money. Neither of them wanted the other to have it.

As far as Bella knew, Ethan didn't want the place anyway. God knew she didn't. Too many memories. Too many reminders of how happiness could drift away like autumn leaves falling from their trees, to be trampled underfoot and turned to dust.

Inside, late afternoon light slanted off the lake and through the wall of windows and glass doors that led out onto the porch, filling the room with a warm glow and turning the wood to a gleaming deep honey. This had always been her favorite time of day here. She loved the play of the sunbeams on the water as the sun sank. She could sit on an Adirondack chair on the porch for hours, sipping a tart chardonnay, listening to the outboard motor hum of boats on the water and the occasional shout of an enthusiastic skier. Other than that, the rustle of the wind through the trees, the chatter of a squirrel or call of a bird was all that broke the peaceful silence.

If the sliding glass door was open, she might also have heard Ethan banging pots and dishes in the kitchen as he made dinner. They tended to make simple meals when they came out here for the weekend: pasta *aglio e olio* with a salad of tomato and freshly shaved Parmesan. Omelets stuffed with feta and basil and garlic. Grilled chicken, the occasional steak. Fruit and cheese for dessert.

Bella shook her head, trying to dislodge the remembrances. She shouldn't have come.

And yet she stepped inside, shut the door behind her.

The cabin wasn't tiny, but it was a comfortable size for a weekend getaway. The open plan meant that the view from the door was straight out the back to the lake. In the living room, simple Mission-style furniture gathered around a stone fireplace. Over the mantle was a painting of a proud buck (they had joked about hanging a deer's head, but neither of them had really meant it), and boldly striped Indian-woven blankets were draped over the sofa and chairs.

To the right was the doorway to the master bedroom and bath, and a wide wooden staircase that led upstairs to the loft, with bedrooms and a bathroom for guests.

The kitchen was along the back as well, open to the living room, with windows looking out on the lake and the tangle of trees to the north: stately pines, poplars, birches. If she woke before Ethan, Bella had enjoyed the early morning solitude of brewing coffee and watching the shadows diminish; more often than not, however, she had been the night owl, watching the stars prick the sky and the moon leave a shimmering trail on the water as she nursed a brandy and put away the dishes.

Bella set her purse on the small half-round table by the front door, hung her blazer on a wooden peg just above.

Too familiar.

Even with the realtor's changes, the place felt like home. Oh, it felt bare—no magazines on the coffee table that they'd bring to read and never get around to (same as home), no stack of empty wine bottles to recycle, no towels draped over the porch railing to dry after a late-morning swim.

Or a late-night swim.

She sat down hard on the sofa, half-feeling like an intruder, half-feeling lost and very, very small.

Remember when they would sneak down to the lake, under the full moon? They'd shuck what little clothes they had on— their wardrobe was so much simpler than when they were in the city—and dive into the water (chilly even in the height of summer), stifling their squeals, laughing breathlessly.

Ethan would complain that he'd lost all feeling between his legs, but it wouldn't be long before it became apparent that he was feeling very well indeed. His cock would rise, hot in the cool water.

They'd be lucky if they made it to the raft before the groping started in earnest. Sometimes they'd just head back to the shore, lie on the soft grass above the beach. Moonlight would shimmer in Ethan's dark hair, and she wouldn't be able to see his expression, but she'd hear his voice, rough with passion. He'd tell her how beautiful she was, how sexy, and he'd follow the droplets of water on her pale flesh with his tongue.

Down from her neck, to the hollow where it met her shoulder. Laving away the moisture, teasing her sensitive flesh there. He'd spent more time there than was strictly necessary to catch all the drops, knowing how it made her press up against him, nails digging into his back, whispering harsh and incoherent into his ear.

Only then would he move down, along her collarbone, to everywhere but the center of her breasts until she moaned in unfulfilled need.

He'd capture one of her taut nipples—puckered and dark from the cold swim—between his lips. God yes. Her back would arch; she'd be arching her hips from the moment he started suckling and grazing with his teeth. She'd get so wet, so hot and slick, but he'd linger there, entranced by how hard her nipples would get, how ripe and juicy (he would murmur against her flesh, as if he were drunk, drunk on the lust of her).

A teasing tongue in her navel, flicking out the water there, and then he'd move farther down. A quick nip on her hip bone, a nuzzle against her inner thigh. Her fingers would take the place of his mouth—seeing her pleasure herself always drove him a little mad—and then he'd find the true source of moisture, like Galahad succeeding in his quest for the Grail. He'd taste her, with a low groan that sent more shivers through her, before parting her folds and taking mercy on her.

Strokes of his tongue against her clit, so knowing and true.

He knew just how to touch her, urging her higher and higher, keeping her on edge until...

Overhead the stars would wheel and blur as she surrendered to the sensations. She whirled through space on the spasms of her climax, tethered to the earth only by Ethan's hands and mouth and touch on her.

Lying on the sofa (where, yes, they'd also made love—there wasn't a spot in the cabin where they hadn't succumbed to heady, freeing passion), Bella slid her hand under her skirt and found her slick lips, her engorged clit. Riding on the memories, she brought herself to orgasm.

Moisture stained her fingers even as tears stained her face.

She hadn't known, the last time they'd made love here, that it would be the last time.

And now the cabin was for sale.

Memories for sale: cheap.

Bella hadn't meant to fall asleep on the sofa, clutching a pillow and dampening another with her tears.

But then, she probably hadn't meant half of what she'd said (or even more than that) in the crimson heat of anger in their last days together. The bitter, nasty arguments in which they'd both used the intimate knowledge they had of each other to wound and cut. The vicious arguments, which had preceded the period of bone-chilling silence, which had preceded the taut, death-knell conversation ending their marriage.

"I suppose we'd be better off apart."

"I suppose we would."

Bella couldn't remember who'd said which sentence. It no longer mattered, anyway.

She woke when she heard a noise. Disoriented, she blinked in the almost-darkness of twilight, unsure where she was, what she heard. The pillow clutched against her chest was damp. She fumbled for a lamp and clicked it on to remember the cabin, the memories.

The door opened, and adrenalin surged. She stood, abruptly, to face the danger.

Her heart twisted, betraying her.

*Ethan.*

"Oh." He stood in the doorway, backlit by the porch light. Still, she knew him from his outline, from the way he carried himself. "I didn't expect..."

"I'm sorry, I didn't..."

They trailed off together. They'd long since run out of things to say; why would now be any different?

Bella broke the silence first.

"I just stopped by to see the cabin one more time. I'll get out of your way now."

He shifted the grocery bag he held to his other hip. "No, there's no rush. I'm sorry I interrupted you. I didn't think you'd be here."

She shrugged, helplessly. "I didn't think you would, either."

He looked wan, she thought. Had he lost weight? His blond hair was neat, but she wondered if it had receded at the temples. He'd been sensitive about the idea. It was the one thing she'd never used against him, even in the cruellest of moments. She never knew why she'd held back. Maybe it was because, even though she knew how the problem gnawed at him, she'd never cared. He'd always looked handsome to her.

Even now.

This silence was awkward. How could you feel awkward with someone you'd loved, someone you'd been intimate with, someone with whom you'd shared everything with for nine years?

"I should go," he said finally.

"No," she said as he turned away. "This is still your cabin as much as it is mine."

The stilted, overly polite interactions they'd had since the decision. All emotion had drained away. They were left with court-document, lawyer-speak, cool pleasantries.

How had it come to this?

He regarded her for a moment, as if gauging the honesty of her statement, before he nodded. "Fine, then. Thanks."

She watched in silence as he carried the bag across the room into the kitchen, then back to pick up a sleeping bag he'd left on the porch.

"I should go," she said, realizing only after the words had left her mouth that she'd echoed his.

He pursed his lips, in the way he did when he was considering something. She'd forgotten that until just now.

"Really, it's okay," he said finally. "This is still just as much your place as mine. Let's not make it worse. Would you...like a glass of wine?"

She did, very much. More than she wanted to admit.

"A little would be nice, yes. What did you bring?"

It was something from South Africa, a heady merlot. Her mouth watered at the memory of it. "One glass, then."

"Steak. I confess I was going for man comfort food," he said as he poured. "Women go for chocolate, men go for cow. I've got potatoes, salad fixings. There's more than enough for two."

She swirled the wine in the glass, noticing how it didn't cling. That seemed like a lesson she should learn.

She'd never been one for lessons or following directions or orders. She supposed it was her downfall, that stubbornness.

"So why did you come back?" she asked.

He dashed salt and pepper over the thick steak, not looking at her. "Nostalgia, I suppose. One last night in the cabin. You?"

"Same thing, although I just wanted to stop by." She leaned against the counter, shook her head. "I guess I didn't really comprehend that it was for sale, that it wouldn't be ours any longer, until I saw the sign."

"Same here." He ran water over the vegetables in the colander. "Look, Bella, I…"

"I know," she said. "Me, too." She looked down at the wine, but it didn't give her any easy answers. There probably weren't any. She looked back up. "I'd like to stay for dinner. What can I do?"

She rinsed off two baking potatoes—he'd grabbed a bag of them at the store—and pricked them with a fork, smelling the earthy scent of them. She was, she realized, famished.

Astonishing, really, how easy it was to fall into the old routines. The two of them in the kitchen, she being sous chef to his head cook. But at the same time, it was also awkward; they'd lost the automatic way they'd had of moving around each other, not bumping into each other (unless they really wanted to, sharing a laughing kiss before turning back to the task at hand).

Somewhere along the line, they'd lost that.

It had been a gradual transition. Bella couldn't look back and find one instant, one moment when everything turned. It came down to a series of missteps, and before they noticed the stumbles, it was too late to catch up and right themselves, and the marriage.

Ethan's business had gone under, and although she still had a good job, he stressed about money. He pulled away from her, confided in another woman. It had been a purely emotional relationship, not physical in the least, but for Bella that had cut deeper than if he'd had an affair.

It had been her mistake to fall into bed with someone else.

She and Ethan had argued (again), she'd stayed late at work and then gone out for a drink that had turned into several, followed by a tumble with an acquaintance. She didn't forgive herself by the fact that she'd been tipsy, because it had happened a few more times, until her lover had gone back to his own wife.

It had been a mistake, and it had been the final nail in the coffin.

After that, she and Ethan tried and failed (finally) to reconcile, to come to some middle ground. They were so far apart that they couldn't see the middle. Certainly they couldn't see each other.

Now, she chopped vegetables, crumbled bleu cheese, and tossed a salad, and then they went onto the porch with their wine to wait for the potatoes to bake. Ethan would throw the steaks on at the last minute.

A loon called, low and haunting.

"I hadn't realized until now just how much I'd missed this," she said, indicating with her glass the view of the lake. "It was always so peaceful up here."

"Except that time Jo and Kent brought their nephew with them," Ethan said. "God, he was a terror."

"I don't know how we got through the weekend without killing him," Bella agreed, laughing. "He clogged the toilet, terrorized the chipmunks..."

"...and refused to eat anything except Cocoa Puffs and Spaghetti-Os..."

"...which Kent had to drive half an hour into the village to get..."

"...while Jo cursed his name under her breath for abandoning her."

They were both laughing now, free and easy. Bella couldn't remember the last time it had been so natural to laugh, as if a blockage had cleared in her chest.

"At least we can laugh about it now," she said.

"It's strange, isn't it?" he asked. "How things that seem so awful at the time end up being pretty minor later, when you remember them."

"The blissful haze of memory," she said.

"Natural brain defense mechanism. You know, Bella, I—"

The kitchen timer pinged.

"I have to put the steaks on," he said.

She set the table, then abandoned the porch to walk barefoot in the cool grass to the wild area nearby where wildflowers clustered. When he brought the plates out, he nodded at the simple arrangement she'd made in an old jam jar. "Nice."

It was the clear lake air, she decided, that made her so hungry. The steak was perfect, the potatoes crisp on the outside and steaming soft inside, the salad a light counterpoint to the rest of the meal. It all went down nicely with the wine.

Shadows grew, the sky turning a gorgeous shade of deep blue. Across the table, Bella watched Ethan, noting the circles beneath his eyes.

Surprised, she found herself wanting to smooth them away with her fingers, ease him into a healing sleep.

Now, where had that come from? The wine, probably.

But the wine didn't explain why she'd stayed for dinner, why she'd put flowers on the table.

Nothing, it seemed, made sense anymore.

They did the dishes together in silence—what once would have been an awkward or angry lack of discussion now felt companionable. He'd set the timer on the coffee pot before they'd eaten, and the fresh brew filled the cabin with aromatic steam.

He handed her a mug as she sat on the sofa. He'd remembered how she liked it—light on the cream, two sugars. Before he joined her, he lit the fat new cranberry-red candle on the coffee table.

"Jane's not going to like that," Bella said of the realtor.

He blinked, as if he hadn't considered that until now. Then he shrugged. "So I'll buy another."

Typical Ethan. His ability to brush off the details that didn't really matter had infuriated her at the end.

But they hadn't always, had they? At the beginning, hadn't she loved his casual way of cutting through what wasn't important, to find the core of what was?

The melancholy that settled over her, she couldn't entirely blame on the wine, either.

"Ethan, I—"

"Bella, I—"

They spoke at the same time, stopped, laughed, this time with hesitance. The easy humor from supper was gone.

"Ladies first," he said.

She fortified herself with a sip of hot coffee, then cradled the mug in her hands, forcing herself to look at Ethan rather than down.

"I...I just wanted to say that I'm sorry." She hadn't known exactly what she'd wanted to say until now, yet now it was very clear what she needed to say. "The affair. It was stupid. It was the stupidest thing I've ever done. I didn't care about it. I just reacted badly to you confiding in someone other than me."

They weren't sitting close, but when he shifted to face her more fully, his knee was an inch from her thigh. They both stared at the tiny gap for a moment.

"I thought it was because I'd failed," he said finally.

"What?"

"I thought you had the affair because I'd failed. I know you were making enough for us to get by, but I couldn't handle not contributing." He shook his head. "I'd lie awake at nights, stressing about money, wondering how you could stay with someone who wasn't good enough to provide. So when you..."

"Why didn't you tell me?" she asked. "I pulled away because you pulled away. You wouldn't let me in, and it hurt so bad when you shared what you were feeling with someone else instead of me. Like I wasn't important enough to you to confide in, to give you support."

"I'm so sorry," he said. "I shouldn't have shut you out. I didn't even realize I was doing it."

She set her mug down. "We're a pair of fucking idiots."

He snorted.

"No, I mean it," she said. "Why didn't we talk about this then?"

"We were too busy blaming," he said. "As I recall, there was a fair bit of shouting, too."

She saw him hesitate, guessed what he wanted to do. Prayed he would.

And he did, taking her hands in his.

"The blissful haze of memory," he said. "We're both way too stubborn. You'd think the marriage counselor could have gotten this conversation out of us, but no..."

She freed one hand and picked up her coffee. The caffeine wasn't helping the dizzy rush in her head from the wine and the conversation.

"Do you remember," Ethan said, "the first night we stayed here?"

"You mean when we couldn't even make it to the bedroom?"

He nodded. His eyes never leaving hers, he took the mug from her hand and set it back on the table.

She didn't let him lean all the way in to kiss her.

She met him halfway.

The kiss was tentative, which was so unlike him that she almost drew back. But the taste of him, which she'd almost forgotten until now and had never stopped missing, was almost too much to bear, and she couldn't pull away.

It was that, she guessed, that emboldened him. When she responded, his touch grew more sure. He drew her in and she went willingly, the feel of his tongue against hers triggering the warm glow of arousal that she knew would soon smolder, ignite, and finally consume her.

So familiar, and yet so foreign. Each step along the unlit path brought back hints of remembrance, like sweet déjà vu.

She traced his biceps, ran her hands down his back, feeling the muscles flex. He bit gently on her lower lip, and she gasped, the thrill streaking down between her legs. She was already wet, wetter even than when she'd masturbated earlier. His touch had always done that to her.

How had she gone so long without this?

He grazed his teeth along the line of her throat as she plucked at his shirt buttons. She didn't get all of them, but she couldn't wait any longer, splaying her hands across his smooth chest, lightly tracing her nails over his nipples until he groaned. He took one of her hands and guided it down to his crotch, pressing her palm against the bulge there, showing her just how excited she made him. Her clit shivered in response.

Fleetingly, she wondered where this was leading. Oh, to sex, obviously, but wasn't sex with your ex supposed to be anathema? Tacky, even? (Not that he was her ex just yet, but as good as.) She ignored that thought, pushed away all thoughts.

They didn't matter. What mattered was his hands and lips and tongue on her, and her hands and teeth on him, and the need they shared.

He tugged her shirt free and pulled it over her head, and by the time he'd tossed it away she had already made good headway toward removing her bra, popping the front hook and shrugging out of it. His eyes were dark in the candle flame, but she could imagine the hunger in them before he dipped his head to suckle.

So good. She arched her back in response as he teased her, drawing each bud between his lips, flicking with his tongue, biting just enough to make her squirm and beg.

Beg him not to stop. Beg him for more.

She dipped a hand between her legs, under her panties, and soaked her fingers, then spread the moisture on her nipples for him to savor.

"So sweet," he murmured. "Bella...I have to taste you for real."

They didn't even bother removing her long, loose skirt. She hiked it up while he slid the now-useless panties over her hips, down her thighs. The scrape of the lace against her skin was almost more than she could bear.

She propped her feet on the coffee table and he knelt between her legs. He breathed in the scent of her until she thought she'd scream. She tangled her fingers in his hair, but didn't really tug—it was an old habit with them, almost a joke. She'd urge, but she'd still let him take the lead, make the decision to finally lean all the way in and swipe his tongue across her lips, bury between her folds, nuzzle against her clit.

When he finally did, she let out a long sigh, feeling like they had both come home.

Then his talented tongue was working its magic, flicking against her swollen bud, stoking the fire. She pressed her head so hard against the back of the sofa that she knew her neck would hurt the next day, but she didn't care. The scorching spiral toward orgasm wound tighter and tighter, the fire consuming her until she screamed her release.

Ethan didn't give her much time to recover, and she didn't blame him. He shucked off his pants and underwear, and she saw how hard he was, tasted the moisture that seeped from the tip of his cock. He groaned as she did, but pulled her away a moment later, telling her he needed to be inside her.

She had no argument for that.

He urged her up, and she knelt on trembling legs to face the back of the sofa. He wasted little time sliding into her, and no matter how long it had been, she welcomed him, knowing now just how much she'd missed him. His hands were full of her breasts as he pushed into her.

She felt his thrusts grow staccato, knew he was close. She welcomed that, too, because she was already on edge again herself, from the rake of his cock deep inside her and the pressure of his hands on her nipples. She felt herself clamp down, and then she tumbled into another orgasm, pulsing along the length of him. Dimly she heard his own shout as he came with her.

Eventually they roused themselves, although it was largely so Ethan could check whether the bottle of brandy they always tucked into a back cabinet was still there. It was.

They sipped and talked, long into the night, long past the three-quarter moon's shimmer on the water. Eventually they staggered to the bedroom, spread the sleeping bag he'd brought onto the bed, and made love again. Slower, this time, and more bittersweet, perhaps, as Bella cradled his head in her hands and he buried his face in her shoulder as they came.

They were roused the next morning not by the stream of sunlight across the bed but the sound of the front door being unlocked. Ethan scrambled into pants and shirt, giving Bella time to dive for the bathroom.

She was vaguely amazed she had no hangover. And no heartache.

In the bathroom mirror, she saw that her hair was a tangle, her lips puffy from kisses, and her eyes sparkling from pleasure despite the circles beneath them. She pulled herself together as best she could. She had no idea where her bra had ended up, but there was nothing she could do about that right now. Shirt and skirt would suffice.

She emerged to find Jane, the realtor, clutching bread mix (because the scent of baking bread was a huge lure to buyers) and fresh flowers. Ethan, meanwhile, had Bella's bra clutched behind his back.

Bless his heart.

"Bella!" Jane's astonishment was clear. "You're here, too."

Bella gave a weak wave. "Morning, Jane."

"Well." Jane's voice turned brisk as she went into professional mode. "We'll have to get things cleaned up before the open house starts. There's already a line of cars at the end of the drive. I'll get the bread going. The sofa cushions need to be straightened, and that candle…"

"We appreciate everything you've done for us," Ethan said. "But we've reconsidered, and we've decided not to sell."

"We have?" Bella asked. Her heart rose even as her stomach plummeted, her emotions in a tangle.

"I'm not ready to sell," Ethan said, taking her hand. "That would be selling all the memories we have here. I think we have a chance to make more memories. If you're willing to try, that is."

"It won't be easy," Bella said cautiously. "We've got a lot of work to do. Communication, and all that."

Ethan drew her into his arms. "I realized something. When we're here, we've never had problems talking. We were able to leave our problems behind; this was always a place where nothing else mattered except us."

Bella took a deep breath. "Take down the 'For Sale' sign and cancel the open house," she said to Jane. But it was Ethan she was looking at when she said, "This isn't for sale anymore."

# BLAME IT ON FACEBOOK

Kate Dominic

I smoothed the front of my red silk dress and gazed out the floor-to-ceiling glass windows of my twelfth-floor hotel room. Boats glided by in the marina below. I'd sworn I'd never come back to San Diego. Yet here I was, once again as alone as if I were out in the middle of the vast blue expanse of the Pacific looming beyond the breakwater.

Damn, I was nervous. Despite daily Facebook posts, texts, email, and lately, phone calls, it had been twenty years since I'd seen Eric. I'd changed. I had no doubt he'd changed. The Wonderbra my college sophomore daughter had insisted I buy gave me cleavage I'd never realized I had. Everything was different. And God, when had Melissa gotten old enough to give me dating advice?

Not that I'd ever dated much. Not that she'd remember, anyway. Besides, I'd always considered my legs to be my best asset. I was wearing silk stockings a shade darker than my light summer tan and three-inch heels. My curves were softer now, but I still danced miles of aerobics each week, keeping myself in shape.

Melissa's father had loved seeing me strut across the room in trashy stockings, a slinky top with no bra, and a shockingly short "Do me" skirt. Jerry had been all about visual stimulation, and he loved ripping my clothes off me. Our life together had been a rush of hot lust and youthful immediacy. Hell, maybe we'd just been all about youth. It was so long ago, sometimes the details blurred.

Some things, I'd never forget. After Jerry's memorial service, I'd deliberately cut off contact with his Special Operations buddies. Cutting my ties to their wives and girlfriends had been harder, but I'd done that, too. We'd been family, bonded through history we couldn't begin to describe to people who hadn't been through it. Not that we were allowed to talk about much of anything. There had been days I'd wondered if our grocery lists would end up classified.

When the guys were gone, we helped each other cope with morning sickness and colic, with repairs for our POS cars and day care that never stayed open late enough, and always, with the bone-deep loneliness and fear. I'd been part of a band of sisters who understood the occasional need for immediate over-night babysitting when the guys were home and one of them put his hands on his wife's or girlfriend's hips, looked into her eyes, and they shared a look that let you know they wouldn't be coming up for air until morning.

God, we were so young back then. So naïve and certain we were immortal.

Eight months after Saddam invaded Kuwait, the quick, fero-cious first Gulf War was over. Jerry was dead, I was moving out of base housing as a widow with two small children, and the guys were just getting back. Eric came straight to the house, his hair still wet from his shower. He took me in his arms and held me close, the low murmur of his, "Oh, baby, I'm so sorry," vibrating through my ears.

I clung to him, inhaling the scent of his warm strong body, and knowing in that moment that while I'd survive losing Jerry, I'd never survive going through that kind of loss again. The Special Operations community is small and insular, and the women who've been part of it know the score. Eventually, Eric or others like him would be coming by my civilian apartment, wanting me to be part of their world again. They'd wait, quietly, until I was ready to rejoin them.

I knew I'd never be ready. I packed up the car, hauled the kids and the dog to my hometown in Minnesota, got a business degree, and threw myself into my career and motherhood. And I never looked back. I cut my ties so completely, the only person I kept in contact with was my best friend, Janelle, and even that wasn't by choice. She simply refused to accept my silence, and she had my parents' address. The year Melissa started middle school, I started sending Christmas and birthday cards in return. Eventually, after a tearful phone reunion, Janelle and I started calling each other.

By then, we were both online, so we emailed as well. We rarely discussed her husband, Chris, and by unspoken agreement, she never brought up anybody else from the past. We talked about our jobs and the kids and the books we were reading.

Last year, out of the blue, after years of comfortable correspondence, she sent me a Facebook invitation. The moment I realized what a "friends" list was, I knew my days of peaceful isolation were over.

"Oh, sweetie, I've missed you so! May I please be a FB friend?" This from the woman who'd watched my son while I was in labor with Melissa.

"Hey, toots! It's good to see you!" From Janelle's Chris, who'd helped Jerry rebuild motorcycles and later on carried his body back, though I hadn't found out about that until Melissa was in high school.

Greetings and welcomes. So many friends, so much quiet acceptance. And some conspicuous absences. I didn't ask about those. The guys had all been adrenaline junkies, and several had planned to make careers of the military. There had been so many conflicts in the intervening years. I didn't want to know. Even with the online reunions, I told myself I was going to keep concentrating only on the present. To make my point, I used a real profile picture—then was surprised that several others had, too. With a jolt, I realized their lives allowed that now. They'd moved on as well.

Eric had a cartoon character for his profile picture.

"I miss you."

His friend request caught me off guard, though in retrospect, I'd been half-expecting it. I could almost hear the warm burr of his voice as I clicked Accept. We'd always had an easy friend-ship. And if I was honest with myself, I had to admit he'd been easy on the eyes. Eric was tall and slender, with dark blond curls and dancing blue eyes. He was usually laughing, he didn't under-stand the concept of "subtle," and he had the most gorgeously pinchable butt. Not that I'd ever pinched him, but Janelle and the other girls sure had. There'd been a few times I'd been ticked at Jerry and wondered "what if" I hadn't been married, and if Eric hadn't had that constant string of girlfriends. But, hell, my fantasies had never gone beyond innocent daydreams.

I wondered what Eric looked like now. Sharing status updates segued into private messages. I was surprised to hear he'd never married. He'd known through Janelle that I was still single, but he said he was surprised that even my occasional dating had never gotten particularly serious.

"The kids were around." My face heated as I typed. "I didn't want to set a bad example by staying out all night with someone they knew I didn't care that much about."

I could almost hear Eric's low chuckle, see his eyebrows rise as he looked knowingly at his computer screen.

"Are the kids there now?"

He knew they weren't. As always, he kept things light and friendly. But the occasional humorous innuendo in his status updates and the respectful but blunt comments in his private posts made it clear he was as aware as I was that the heat simmering between us was gradually flaring hotter.

*Embers*, I thought, amazed at my own silly romanticism. *Embers fanned by every word whispering between us.* I was being courted over the Internet and was shocked to discover I enjoyed it. A few months later, though, when I found out I was unexpectedly being sent to San Diego on business, I knew I had to make some hard decisions—ones I wasn't sure I was ready to make. San Diego was reality, not the Internet.

The bastard sent me roses. Roses, dammit! A dozen long-stemmed, deep red roses so fragrant their perfume filled my living room. The card's message was simple, elegant black letters on crisp white card stock. "Wear red for me. Eric"

"No fair," I whispered, tears streaming down my face. I had no idea how he knew about the trip. No doubt, I thought angrily, it was somehow related to whatever job he now had that kept his profile picture a cartoon. But by then, I knew in my heart it didn't matter anymore. I booked my flight and made reservations at one of the tower hotels down by the marina. Then I went shopping for a dress, and shoes, and lingerie that would keep me feeling sexy even if I never let him see it. I told myself that was more reality than I had to deal with yet. It was my choice. But I still got my hair cut and bought new perfume and, God help me, some condoms. And when it was time to pack, I tucked one of those damn roses in my suitcase and headed for the airport.

*"Is he there yet?"* Melissa texted as I checked my lipstick one last time.

*"I'm heading to the lobby now."*

I paused and added, *"Turning my phone to vibrate, Miss Nosey. I want PRIVACY this evening."*

*"Pouting, but happy for you. Go for it, Mom. I love you!"*

*"Love you, too. Good night."*

I set my volume to vibrate and tucked my phone in my clutch. Then I took a deep breath, set the rose on the bed, and headed off to the elevator.

As soon as the lobby doors opened, I saw him. Eric was standing opposite the elevator, leaning nonchalantly against the wall exactly where I'd expected him to be. It was the vantage point that let him, quietly and unobtrusively, see everyone and everything going on in the entire room and outside the huge glass doors. Either old habits died hard, or he was still in the same line of work.

He'd seen me, too. He smiled as he straightened and started toward me. He was still slender, his muscles still moving with the same quiet strength beneath his dark linen suit. His hairline had receded a bit, the style well cut, but not military short anymore. A light blue shirt set off the color of his eyes and crows' feet crinkled at the corners of his eyes. And oh, he was smiling. I'd so missed his smile.

I met him halfway, my hands out to take his. But when his arms slid around me, somehow it was right. I slipped into his embrace like I'd never left, and we stood there in the middle of the lobby, tears streaming down my face as we clung to each other.

"Oh, baby, I've missed you. It's so good to see you again."

His voice wavered, and I smiled into the warmth of his chest. "I've missed you, too." My laugh was shaky. "It's a good thing I'm not wearing mascara, or I'd have ruined your shirt."

He inhaled as my mouth opened—I could almost hear the words between us. *Then the shirt would have to come off.*

But neither one of us spoke. Instead he led me to a quiet corner where I could dry my eyes and blow my nose. I tried to excuse myself to go to the ladies room, to splash cold water on my face, but Eric shook his head, trailing the side of his knuckle down my cheek.

"You're beautiful just the way you are. I don't want to waste another minute without you." He nodded toward the door. "My car's outside. Let's go to dinner."

He held out his hand. His eyes held mine, and they didn't look away. In that moment, I knew I'd made up my mind. I squared my shoulders, put my hand in his, and we left.

The restaurant was only a few blocks away, still on the waterfront. The sun was setting. Lights twinkled on the boats moving slowly past the restaurant's huge bay windows. "On the recommendation of a friend," Eric ordered swordfish and delicate pasta, the perfectly steamed house vegetables, and a light white wine. We each had a single glass, and spumoni for dessert.

I knew dinner was delicious. But my attention was riveted to the mesmerizing voice of the man whose absence, I was quickly realizing, had been a hole in my life for almost twenty years. Each laugh, each stroke of his finger over the back of my hand or along my palm, was like a salve seeping in to fill the voids inside me with color and sound and even the damn aromas of the appetizer samples he held out to me on the end of his fork. God, I'd missed him.

We spent hours and two pots of coffee filling in the three-dimensional details that online communication could never quite complete. No matter what the subject, my thoughts always came back to the compelling blue eyes of the man beside me. I was coming to realize that every post, every status update and private message, had been a form of foreplay between us.

Now every touch, every smile and whisper, was taking our intimacy one step closer. My pussy tingled, and my nipples were hard enough I expected Eric couldn't help noticing. More than once, his hand slipped beneath the table. I envisioned the firm, thick erection I'd occasionally seen tenting the front of his jeans all those years ago, now pressing up into the expensive dark linen of his beautiful blue suit. I got even hotter, and more nervous, imaging his cock filling for me.

"God, even these mints are good!" I laughed to distract myself when he popped one of the creamy pink squares into my mouth.

He wiggled his eyebrows at me. "Janelle will be pleased to know you like her favorite 'fancy restaurant.'"

I tipped my head, running my finger along the side of the hand cupping my face. "She knew you were bringing me here," I said quietly.

His eyes never left mine. "Yes. I told her I wanted to take you someplace special—someplace neither of us had ever been." Eric had always been direct. No hedging. No bullshit. I nodded and kissed the place I'd just touched.

"Thank you."

The waiter came by with more coffee, but Eric just kept looking at me. "Would you like to dance off some of this caffeine?"

There was a wealth of meaning in his eyes, not subtle, but not pushing either. Inquiry, arousal, and patience. Infinite patience that was, perhaps, getting ready to change to something else.

I took a deep breath, then I shook my head and let go of his hand. "No. I want to go back to the hotel. With you."

His eyes never left mine as he pulled out his wallet and handed the waiter a wad of cash. Eric guided me outside, his hand resting on the small of my back as we waited for the valet to bring the car. The music wafting over from the dance floor was just loud enough to provide an excuse not to converse. I wondered if that was for the best. I was getting really nervous. My palms weren't the only parts of my body that were damp.

We'd barely left the parking lot, though, when Eric pulled over to the curb. He turned, his arm moving to the back of the seat as he looked directly at me.

"Are you sure about this?" he asked quietly. "I've waited for you for years. I can wait longer if you need me to."

For a moment, I wondered if he'd changed his mind. The hours we'd spent talking online just weren't the same as being together in person. But his hand was shaking, ever so slightly, and his voice wasn't completely steady. I wasn't the only one nervous as hell here.

I licked my lips and turned to lean against the door, letting my Wonderbra do its cleavage magic as I stretched my leg just enough to open my thighs beneath the clinging silk of my skirt. I was so wet I half-expected he could smell me.

"Don't you want me?"

His pupils dilated, his nostrils flaring as his eyes flicked quickly to my breasts, lingered, then slid purposefully down and back up my body. He threw his head back against the seat and laughed.

"Christ, woman! I want you so badly I'm about to come in my pants." His voice came out hoarse in the quiet of the car. "Do you want me?"

Yes. The answer was yes. I kept my eyes on his, knowing at

that moment, I was going to let him see my lingerie.

"I'm wearing crotchless panties. Just in case." I couldn't stop the flush heating my face. "Not that I expected you to ever know that."

He closed his eyes and groaned, his knuckles white as he took deep, bracing breaths. When he finally looked at me, his eyes smoldered. He smiled crookedly.

"After all this time, it would be really embarrassing to come before we got our clothes off."

"Drive!" I laughed. He drove.

My cell vibrated. Melissa. I turned it off. Eric's cell vibrated. He pulled it out, grimacing as it slipped from his fingers and onto the seat beside me.

"Would you please turn that fucking thing off!"

I glanced at the Caller ID as I pressed the button. "J C Home?"

"Janelle and Chris. And that would be Janelle. Chris would not be calling me now!"

I giggled like a schoolgirl. "Does the whole world know we're going out tonight?"

"Yes, dammit!" He looked at me, both of us sobering at the same time. "I'm sorry if that bothers you. God, I hope it doesn't! I've been in love with you for so long. I feel like some gawky-assed teenager tripping over his words."

He took a deep breath, letting it out slowly as he realized what he'd said.

"Shit. I hadn't meant to say that yet. The L-word, I mean. But it's true, dammit, and I won't take it back. I love you. I want to marry you. And I'm making a total fucking mess of this conversation!" He slammed his hand against the wheel. "Fuck!"

We were pulling into the hotel. Eric turned toward the parking structure. I put my hand on his arm and said, "Valet.

Now." He whipped the wheel to the left and into the circle in front of the main entrance. I released my seat belt, braced my hand on his thigh, and leaned over him until my lips were just above his.

"I love you, too. Yes, I'll marry you. I'm out of my fucking mind, but it's true, and I'm scared to death. Take me upstairs and make love to me until I'm not afraid anymore."

I fell back in the seat, shaking like a leaf. If I looked anything like he did, the valet was getting one hell of an education in what "deer in the headlights" looked like.

"Fair enough," he choked. And tripped trying to get out of the car without taking his seatbelt off.

I don't remember getting to the elevator. I was in his arms when the door closed, our tongues tangling coffee and mint-laced kisses as he ground his erection into my belly.

"Security cameras," he gasped as he came up for air.

I wrapped my leg around him, the wet silk of my dress rubbing against my pussy. "Don't care." Then we were kissing again.

The bell dinged and he broke free, panting as the elevator door opened. He pulled me down the empty hall, pressing me against the wall as he slid the keycard through the slot. Suddenly his hand was beneath the back of his jacket, the butt of a gun showing at his waist.

"Wait here." He ducked quickly inside, scanning the room, checking the bathroom and under the bed before he pulled me in behind him. Then he shoved the door closed and threw all the locks.

"What the hell is your job!" I demanded. I was shocked to realize I didn't really care. I just wanted to know.

"FBI, fifteen years," he growled, tearing his jacket off, throwing it onto the nightstand. He stripped off the weapon harness, checked the safety, and tossed it down on his jacket.

"Are you okay with that?"

"It's better than blowing up crap in the desert," I sighed. "I'll still worry. Are you okay with that?"

"Yup. I'm not doing as much field work these days. I'll tell you what I can, when I can. It's a lot more than we could, back then."

Eric was looking out the window, still breathing hard, his gaze calculating. He pulled a straight-backed chair out from the desk and set it in front of the window. I have no idea where the condom came from, but there was one on the seat of the chair. He turned on a low light in front of the window and held out his hand to me.

"I want to see you this first time. Really see you. Are you okay with that?"

I nodded, reaching for the zipper at the side of my dress.

"Leave it."

I quirked my eyebrow at him, but I left my dress zipped and walked over to take his hands. The glow from the light turned the glass doors to the balcony into quasi-mirrors, reflecting the room while still letting in the twinkling lights from the marina in the darkness below. Eric slid his fingers up my arms, then he was holding my head to his, his kisses hungry now, still soft but with an underlying desperation that had me quickly running my tongue over the insides of his lips. When I sucked his tongue, he groaned, his hard-on so stiff against me I felt my juices trickling down my thigh.

"Undo my pants," he growled, one hand sliding down to cup my breast. As I tugged his zipper down, the side of my dress parted. His hand was against my bare skin, stroking a trail of fire. His belt clunked to the floor, and his bare hip was against my hand. No underwear. I hadn't expected any.

"I can't wait," he growled against my lips.

"Now," I panted. "Hurry." I reached for the condom and met his hand.

"I'll do it. If you touch me, I'll come."

He stepped out of his pants and sheathed himself, breaking the kiss again to move in back of me. He sat and pulled me to straddle him, my back to his chest, my thighs spread wide over his, the open slit in my panties exposed. My skirt fell between us as he lowered me onto his lap.

"We have a problem," I laughed breathlessly.

"No problem," he panted. The silk of my skirt rasped against my pussy lips as he ground me against the hot flesh of his erection. His groan was long and loud. I closed my eyes, relishing the feel of him lowering the top of my dress, of him lifting my breasts out of their confinement to rest on top of the blasted Wonderbra, the cool air helping his talented fingers tease my nipples to rock-hard peaks.

"Look at the window."

Oh, my God. Our full-length reflections gazed back at us from the long sheet of glass. My head rested against Eric's shoulder, his face visible next to mine, my chest arched forward displaying my bare breasts where he toyed with my nipples. I balanced on my heels as his other hand slowly teased my skirt up, over my thighs, over the tops of my stockings. Higher.

"Christ." Eric's hand shook as he raised the shimmering red silk past the lace-framed, neatly trimmed thatch guarding my pussy lips. His fingers spread the sopping lace, slid between the slick, swollen folds, through the glistening dark pink slit to delve deep into my pussy. "Fuck. Now! I need you now! Lift up."

I did, yanking my dress out from under me. Eric braced himself with one hand. He put the other on my waist, gently guiding me down onto his shaft.

"Fuck!" he growled.

Hot. Full. He filled me so perfectly. The thick girth of his shaft was stretching me, filling me as I'd needed to be filled for so very long. I mewled with pleasure, my hands stretched over my head, my fingers gripping his hair as he rocked his hips beneath me.

"I'm gonna come," he panted, his body arching up, his cock surging deep as he wrapped his arms around me. "Dammit! I'm gonna come!" With one hand, he spread my pussy lips. With the other, he rubbed his finger over my clit in the most delicious, most intense circles of my entire life. I screamed as I came, my pussy muscles gripping and squeezing him in glorious, rhythmic spasms of sheer ecstasy as he roared and bucked up into me. My pussy juice squirted over his hand and I screamed again, clenching him ferociously as he surged and thrust his cock harder, deeper into me.

And he stayed hard. My whole body was trembling as his fingers kept stroking, driving me right back up.

"Again," he growled. "Rock your hips against me."

I did, shuddering as his cock pressed back and forth inside me, deep and hard into places that were orgasms waiting to happen.

"I want to come again," I panted, grinding against him.

"You will, baby," he laughed, "as often as you want." He moved his hand up to my nipples, cupping them and squeezing the hard buds between his thumbs and forefingers. "Use your beautiful, strong legs to lift up on those gorgeous heels, just a little bit." He shuddered as I lifted. "Not too far. That's it. Just enough so we're both feeling your luscious, hot pussy riding my cock."

It felt good. Oh, God, it felt so good!

"P-put your f-fingers, on my c-clit," I panted, clenching my pussy muscles around him, squeezing as I lowered myself, squeezing again as I raised back up.

"In a minute, baby." His voice was a low, sexy growl that made my pussy cream even harder. "I'll touch you again when your pussy is ready. When your clit's so sensitive you scream when I touch it."

He was as good as his word. He raised and lowered me on his cock, fucking me over him while he played with my nipples, getting all those special spots deep inside me so sensitized I was almost going to come from that touch alone.

"Please," I wailed. "Please, now!"

He pulled me down onto his cock, rocking his hips and parting my pussy lips with one hand.

"Look at the window," he growled. "Look at us."

And he touched his finger to my clit. I screamed as the orgasm washed through me, wailed again and again as his finger circled, my eyes locked on his as he shouted and bucked into me so hard the chair rocked against the floor.

"I love you," he panted as I shuddered in his arms. "Always, baby. I'm yours."

"I l-love you, t-too." It was hard to speak. I couldn't stop shaking. Eric's cock twitched inside me. I shuddered as I came again. And again.

When I finally quit trembling, when my pussy finally quit spasming, Eric stood us up and lifted me into his arms. He stripped me naked and took me to bed. Then he traced the rose over my nipples and licked my pussy until I finally I couldn't stand it anymore. I fell asleep in his arms and when we woke up, I took him into my mouth and loved him with my lips and tongue and throat until he was as wasted as I was.

We made love all night. And in the morning, we called Melissa and Janelle and told them we were engaged. Everybody else found out through their Facebook status updates, because Eric and I cleared our calendars for the rest of the week, turned off our computers and phones, and damn well spent most of that time in bed and getting to know each other again.

We're getting married next year, after he's transferred to the Minneapolis office. We'll use traditional invitations—and at Melissa's instigation, we'll also have a Facebook RSVP option for those who can't break away from their computers, because God help me, we're inviting everybody.

We're even having a somewhat traditional wedding night, though only Eric and I know that. As we left the hotel at the end of our extended holiday, Eric turned to me and asked, "Have you ever had anal sex?"

My blush gave him his answer even before I stammered out, "Um, no."

"Me, either," he grinned. "How about we save that for our wedding night? I know some very interesting things we can do in the interim so we're ready for it."

I looked pointedly at his butt. "Okay."

He rolled his eyes and his face turned a beautiful pink, but then he laughed and shrugged. "All right. Both ways. We can order some toys. Damn. I'll send you a Facebook message."

I had no doubt he would. I couldn't wait to see the innuendo only I'd recognize in his status updates.

# THE DRAFT

Craig J. Sorensen

Sarah could have played it safe and bought a VW bug. Cheap, easy to fix, and they were aplenty.

But there was something about the cockpit of the long-nosed, bright red 1948 MG-TC. Still, the noise that ground up from the engine of the twenty-year-old car as she descended the Sierras told her it was not eager to make the round trip. It groaned as it hit the tarmac of a truck stop near Reno. She reluctantly turned the engine off. She tried to turn the engine over, and it made an evil noise. Yes, it was done.

Sarah gathered her midnight-blue polka-dot dress at the knees and slipped through the tiny right-hand door. She opened the engine compartment, and the black smoke slithered out like a cobra, dancing. She made a pistol shape with her left hand and turned it to the engine, covered her own eyes like a blindfold. "Good-bye, old girl." She made a gun sound.

The sound of "Taps" being played. A broad-chested man with a bit of a belly saluted while rendering a convincing bugle sound. Sarah clasped her hand to her heart until he finished the soulful rendition with a smooth vibrato. "Tell me you know something about cars?"

"Cars you bet. These things, no."

"You don't like my baby?"

"Oh, she looks real nice." The man looked inside the engine compartment, then sniffed. "You were right to put it out of its misery."

"That's me, a real humanitarian."

"Not every little lady thinks so practical." He had the face of an eagle with a hooked nose. Bright, mischievous eyes glowed in the mercury vapor parking lot lights. "Can I buy you breakfast?"

"I can buy my own."

"Fair enough." He walked away.

"Is the food good here?" She took quick steps to cover the distance his sturdy long stride placed between them.

"Ain't heard the old saying 'bout where truckers eat?" He waved at the long line of trucks.

"Guess I have." Sarah caught up. "I can pay, but it doesn't mean I want to eat alone." Funny thing was, she was never bothered by eating alone. He held the door open for her. She waved for him to go, and he shrugged then walked in first.

"I'm Sarah." She extended her right hand as they sat on opposite bright red benches of the booth.

"Dave." He took her hand delicately. The edges of his calluses felt like strips of sandpaper around a leather-smooth palm. His hand swallowed hers; she felt compelled to squeeze hard. "Nice grip, little lady." He shook his thick paw. "So, you always drive so early?"

His reaction made her smile. "Felt like getting an early start."

A broad, blond mustache covered his upper lip, slightly

unkempt, and his cheeks were full. His hair was short, and he had a deep cleft in his broad chin.

A waitress in her mid-thirties approached. She was kind of pretty in thick black-cat glasses. She had an Olive Oyl body that she carried with strange grace. "Well, as I live and breathe. How ya been, Dave darlin'?"

His soft accent begat a warm drawl. "I been good Mary Jo. How 'bout you?"

"Well, just dandy. Ain't seen ya in ages."

"I had a run o' work up and down California. Good to be on the east to west again. The folks is nicer." He winked.

Mary Jo pushed her pencil through her bright blonde hair, piled high enough to stretch a five-foot-seven frame to over six feet. "You want the usual, hon?"

"You know what I like!"

Mary Jo turned to Sarah. "And for your lady friend here?"

"Just acquaintances. A cup of coffee, two poached eggs, and dry toast. Separate checks, please."

Mary Jo popped her gum. "Sure thing, hon." She walked away.

"That's some plain eatin', little lady." Dave lifted his brow.

"I like it fine." Sarah felt a little defensive. She eyed Mary Jo. "Old friend?"

"You meet a lot of people on the road. Some real fine people." Dave's eyes locked briefly on the waitress.

"Your friendship extends beyond ham and eggs."

"Were that true, it would be none of your concern, little lady."

"My name's Sarah, not 'little lady.'"

"Well, you ain't big, Sarah."

Sarah collapsed her fingers over a swelling smile. "I'm a little chubby."

"You're built like a woman."

Sarah pursed her lips.

"You don't like being a woman?"

"I like being a woman just fine."

"Where you headed, little...Sarah?"

"Idaho."

"Big place. Any spot in particular?"

"Nampa."

"Nice town. I can take you as far as Winnemucca." Dave pointed to a new, bright red Peterbilt semi with a sleeper outside the diner.

Sarah had planned to find a Travelodge and a garage in the morning. But she was near broke; that's why she was going back. It wouldn't be her first hitchhike. "You think my car's bad?"

"It ain't good."

Sarah knew it was true. "If you don't mind, I'll take that ride." She eyed the big omelet with home fries and toast with cherry jam that Mary Jo set down in front of Dave.

"I can pay." She picked at her carefully chosen breakfast.

Between orderly but ravenous bites from his plate, he said, "For what?"

"The ride."

"No point. I'm already going that way."

When they left, Dave held the passenger door of his truck open. Sarah paused until he walked away from it. She climbed up and closed the door.

Dave sang along with Hank Williams's "Hey Good Lookin'," his voice a near dead ringer. When the song finished, Sarah tapped the dashboard. "I don't have a radio. You mind if I check the local stations? Catch up with the news?"

"Be my guest, darlin'. A dose of Hank'll keep me going for miles."

She twisted the dial all the way up and back down a couple times, then settled on a station. A song started.

Dave's brow lowered. "What's that?"

"Jimi Hendrix, 'Voodoo Child.'"

"The sound?"

"Huh?"

Dave interpreted the guitar's opening notes deftly.

Sarah grinned. "It's a wah."

"A what?"

"A wah. You push it up and down and it makes a sound. You know, like 'wah, wah.'"

"Wah wah."

"Yeah. You like it?"

"Not particularly."

Sarah turned the dial, but Dave gripped her hand and turned it back. His thick fingers were like kindling, strangely delicate. "Leave it."

"But you don't like it."

"Never know till you see something through." He eased her hand from the radio like lifting a rose. After a couple lousy local commercials over the silence in the cab, the song "Bluebird" played.

Dave nodded. "Now I kind of fancy this one."

"I saw Buffalo Springfield in San Francisco. Good show!"

"Is that where you're coming from?"

"Yeah. Protesting."

"Anything in particular?"

"Huh?"

"Protesting. Anything in particular?" A wry smile. He tapped the steering wheel with his meaty thumbs to the beat of the song.

Sarah covered her grin. "What do you think?"

"Well, there are so many things. Could be burning bras. I hear some gals do that, right?" Dave's cheeks went a bit pink. Sarah liked the color.

She squeezed her polka-dot dress between her full breasts. "With boobs like mine, a bra isn't a statement, it's a necessity."

Dave's blush deepened. He laughed. "Okay, whatcha protesting?"

"The war in Vietnam." Silence except for the song. "I suppose you disagree."

"I don't ponder on it much."

"You should."

The radio signal began to flutter. Sarah turned the knob.

"Not much out here." Dave waved across the still-darkened Nevada desert.

"Yeah, I hate it. It's always the same. So boring."

"No, no, you just gotta know what to look for. You can't insist that every road curve and give you big green pastures and majestic mountains. This desert's beautiful. And these long straight roads, well they're steady, predictable, always going someplace, always been someplace. It's a long, beautiful comfort. And give the desert a long drink, and there's nothing like her."

"I can't get you to say a word about the war, but talk about the desert and you go on for a week."

"It's something I like, little..." One brow lifted. "Sarah."

"You don't feel strongly about our men dying for nothing?" Her voice raised.

He held up his hand. "Now, don't you get your dress in a bundle."

"What the hell is that supposed to mean?"

"I didn't mean nothing bad. Look, I think about getting my shipment to the next destination. Keepin' good tires on my rig and the tanks full, staying one up on the state cops. There are smarter people'n me out there to think on that big stuff."

"It's everyone's concern when people are dying for no reason, Dave."

"Well, then, I'll work on that."

The wry twist of Dave's face made her mad. She looked out the right side of the cab until she could lasso her uncomely grin.

Sarah pumped her fist as she found a radio station. "Got one!" Johnny Cash sang "Folsom Prison Blues." She patted Dave's knee. "Bet you like this one."

Dave stared out front and bit his lip.

"Want me to change it?"

"No, leave it. I do like this one."

She leaned closer, chin on her fingers with a close-lipped smile.

"You got something to say, Sarah?"

"You're passionate about deserts and country music."

"Passionate? I like 'em."

"And yet you don't care about the war?"

"Pardon, darlin'. What I said was, 'I don't give it much thought.'"

"My brother's in Canada."

A long pause. "I hear it's nice this time of year."

"He's a draft dodger, Dave."

"I kinda got that, Sarah."

"Honestly I don't know when you're being serious." She took an errant hair from his shoulder.

His eyes turned just enough to watch her make contact. "Is that so?" The radio signal faded. The cab fell silent again but for the throaty hum of the diesel engine. The horizon to the east started to glow.

"If I were a man and got drafted, I'd go to Canada. What do you say to that?" Sarah turned to face him like a confrontation.

"Well, I'd say, 'Tell your brother I said hey.'"
Sarah covered her mouth as she laughed.
"Why you do that?"
"What?"
"You cover your smile."
"Nothing." A long pause. "It's my teeth."
"You got fine teeth."
"The lowers are uneven."
"Yeah. Ain't they grand?"
"Now you're teasing me."
"Nope."
Sarah smoothed the edges of her dress from her plump waist down her full hips.

Another long silence. Dave continued. "When I was a boy, I fought all the time. Drove my ma and pa nuts. One day Mama says, 'Davey, what you fightin' about now?' I say, 'Well Ma, Johnny say some bad things 'bout you.' Ma says, 'Like what?' I say, 'Like you fat.' 'I am fat. You stupid, boy? Fight for telling o' the truth?' But Dad didn't give me a talkin' to. He just walloped me good. Johnny beat me, Dad beat me, Mama was mad at me." Dave nodded to signal the end of his story.

"So, the point is you should choose your battles."

"Listen. A few days later, Johnny calls Mama fatty again. That time I'd figured out how he beat me, and I walloped him but good. That day on, two times my size and big ol' Johnny crossed the street when he saw me a-comin'."

"I don't get you, Dave."

"I got no more points to make. My fightin' days are over."

She eyed his body language, the way he looked at her in scant periphery. "I bet you were in Vietnam. Bet you weren't even drafted."

The corner of Dave's mouth curled up. His accent again

softened. "So, tell me, you think we were wrong to go to Germany and Japan in World War II?"

"War is wrong."

"So we should have laid down for Hitler and Tojo? Been peaceful and stay out of war?"

"Well—"

"How about Korea. Okay to let the South fall?"

"You don't know that it would have."

"No, and you don't know that it wouldn't have. Let's say it did."

"It wasn't our fight."

"Say your brother gets in a fight. Someone starts a fight with him. You see the person who's fighting him has a gun in the back of his pants, where your brother can't see. You can reach it real easy. Do you grab it? Do you warn your brother? Do you just leave it be and hope for the best?"

"My brother doesn't fight."

"He's got no choice this time."

A deep breath. "It's—it's not the same thing."

"You 'spose?"

"I thought you didn't give these things too much thought."

"Just makin' repartee. Answer the question."

"Repartee." Sarah snorted and looked away.

"Answer the question."

"I'd grab the gun, but that's different." She kept her eyes away.

"Knew it." He nudged her elbow gently.

"Don't be so smug. Now you answer me something." She turned back to him.

"Shoot." Dave pointed one finger out toward the desert and made a realistic gun sound complete with long echo.

Sarah grabbed her mouth, then dropped her hand and

allowed her smile to echo as well. "Okay. Say your house is on fire. You're in your room on the first floor, your two kids are asleep in their bedrooms on the third floor, while some adult guests are in the basement."

"I got no wife, no kids, Sarah."

"Play along, Dave, there will be a prize at the end."

He snorted. "I like prizes."

"Do you save the guests, or your kids?"

"Maybe I save the adults, and they help me save my kids."

"But what if you head for the basement, and the fire spreads beyond control. You manage to get the adult guests out, but at what cost?"

"Well, me and the guests line up by the kids' windows and have them jump into our arms."

"Your kids are twenty-two and nineteen respectively, and owing to your big-boned wife tip the scales at 270 pounds each."

Dave howled a deep laugh that nearly shook Sarah's eardrums loose. Amidst laughs he said. "Well, I'm pretty strong."

"Y'all ain't that strong." She conjured a convincing drawl.

"Of course I'd save my kids."

"I knew it!"

"Don't be so smug." Dave looked into the side mirror. "Goddamn. I hate that. Pardon my cursing."

"I heard worse. What's wrong?"

"Guy's drafting."

"Drafting?"

"Yeah, they get up real close and the draft from the trailer pulls them along. Makes me nervous as hell."

Sarah looked away.

"Don't tell me you do that."

She shrugged.

"You know what happens if I gotta stop quick? I saw it happen to another trucker on the road to Stockton. Bigger car than yours, and it wasn't just the driver of the car. She had her..." Dave bit his lip hard. "There was a kid." He looked away and wiped each cheek with his thumb.

"I—I'm sorry." She patted his shoulder.

"Just don't draft, Sarah."

Sarah curled her legs toward him while he studied the mirror. "Okay."

He reached toward the shifter, and his fingers grazed Sarah's bare knee. His hand jerked back. "Pardon."

"For what?"

"Your leg. I mean, it's a fine...it's, uh, real smooth and all. But I didn't mean to...aw hell." That wonderful color lit up his full cheeks. He turned back to the mirror and upshifted until the car appeared from the void behind the truck and passed him.

"It's okay." Sarah edged a little closer to him. Her knee pressed his hip.

Dave squeezed the gearshift tightly.

After a long silence, Sarah resumed, "I think we're spending too much time worrying about other people's gardens. Not tending to our own."

Dave sighed. "Yeah, I can see you draftin' out there on the highway."

"Bet you think women should be seen, not heard."

"No, I just don't see things the same."

"Really?" A hint of sarcasm.

Dave studied the road closely. "You ask a man who's been in hell if he's happy to be in a garden with a few weeds, he's libel to say a big 'yes.'"

"What hell have you been in, Dave?"

"It's just an observation. More repartee."

"It's more than that."

Sarah rested her hand on the top of the seat just behind Dave's shoulder. "You have a nice face."

Dave blushed deeply and looked away.

Sarah grinned. "And you gave me a hard time for covering my smile. You're a traditional man."

"You 'spose?"

"Can't you give a straight answer?"

"You didn't ask a question."

"No, I guess I didn't."

"Standing up for what you believe is good. I'm just a little further down the road in this life than you. Maybe I seen a few things, done a few things, that bring a different light. Speaking of, there's a pretty sunrise about to lift. I most always stop for the sunrise. I drive the night so I can see the morning come." Dave navigated into the next truck stop. He positioned on edge of the parking lot with the cab facing due east, toward the soft wash of vermilion on the naked desert.

"Where were you that sunrises became so important, Dave?"

"What you mean became?"

"Don't toy with me."

He shook his head. "You're a handful."

"Yup. Answer the question."

A long pause. "A place where a man can think through every mistake he made. A place where a man can learn to use his voice like a tape recorder. A place where a man can taste a steak in his mind while scraping scraps of rotten rice up in his fingers. Learn all the things that got past him when he was busy being an idiot fool."

Sarah's knees pressed tighter to Dave's hip. She traced her fingers on his thick shoulder. "Where?"

Spoken softly, "Vietcong prison camp."

"Sorry, that must have been—"

"It's going to be a magnificent sunrise." Dave reached toward her face and waited. She nodded and he stroked her full cheeks, then traced her slim lips with his rough thumb. He whispered, "I may not be looking at that sun when it comes. You're too beautiful."

Sarah started to cover her smile, didn't, and rested her head on his shoulder. She lifted her mouth to Dave. After a pause, Dave dipped his sweet-salty tongue in her mouth. He traced her teeth, then the bottom of her tongue, then around the top. "You taste so fine, Sarah."

She'd never felt a kiss so deep in her body. "May I?" Sarah nodded toward the sleeper behind them.

"Make yourself at home."

She kicked off her shoes and crawled in. She reached for the tie at her waist. "Remember? I said there would be a prize."

He grabbed her hand fast. "That's more'n a prize."

The way he looked at her, the way he said it, made it hard for her not to gasp. It was the time of free love, sexual liberation, and cast in that light, this was a prize, pure and simple. She was sure of it, right up to the moment. She let go of the bow and relaxed her hand into his. "So you never had, just sex for the fun of it, Dave?"

Dave looked out the front of the cab at the growing strip of light. "That's none of your business."

"You have."

"Appetites go strong when a man ain't fed. Sometimes it's hard not to gorge. Don't make it right, and the bellyache after tells you so."

Sarah reached her hand back in the cab and turned his face toward her. "I want to gorge, bellyache be damned." She reached for the tie again. He didn't stop her. She unbuttoned her dress. It fell open.

Dave cleared his throat. Sarah reached into the cab and tried to turn his face to her.

He held fast. "You know, we're in Winnemucca. This is where we...go our separate ways."

"I know." She shook her shoulders. The dress fell away to fully expose her bright white bra and panties. "Ever made love in a sunrise?"

Dave shook his head. "Can't says I have."

"Then you ain't lived, Dave." She pulled his chin again. Now he looked.

His eyes roved up and down her hungrily. "Oh lord."

"Join me." She unclasped her bra, shrugged her shoulders, and her full breasts relaxed. She traced finger and thumb along the top of her panties.

"Oh lord, Sarah."

She could see the bulge in his jeans plainly though his groin was angled away. She pulled down the panties.

The sun emerged fully. Dave didn't look at it. He stayed on Sarah, then jumped into the sleeper. He fumbled with his clothes like a teenager, his first chance at sex. Their limbs formed shadows on the back wall of the sleeper.

"I'm hungry." Dave crouched down in a small parcel at one end of the sleeper, his face turned up, eyes locked in hers. He pressed his face to her clit.

"Oh!" Sarah had a few men do this and it made her feel awkward. It was so intense a sensation, and so personal a place. She let out a gasp as Dave flicked her clit with his tongue. She grabbed the plain white sheets in her fists. Her voice overpowered the rise and fall of diesel engines nearby.

Dave's glossy chin ascended from between her legs, a huge

grin across it. "You're delicious, Sarah."

"I'm hungry too." She motioned for him to lie next to her, facing the other direction. She pulled his cock to her mouth. The tip was beautiful and silky soft. The thick veins curled like vines atop the rigid shaft, and she could not get enough of studying him, taking him as deep as she could into her mouth then tonguing every inch of him. Each time she focused on its base and flicked his tight balls, she felt him jerk.

He rolled her body onto his chest and split her knees as wide as they would go. His tongue was powerful, insistent, unrelenting. She was overcome by a huge, full-body orgasm, her mouth was slack on his flagpole cock. Her limbs tingled and her waist shuddered in time. She tasted him again, but again lost control when a second orgasm washed over her.

She tried her best to overcome him with her mouth. When she managed to take him fairly deep, he became still for a moment, but his fingers and mouth were so capable, all she could do was try to keep up with what was happening in her. The words replayed in her mind. *A place where a man can taste a steak in his mind*...Oh, the things Dave must have thought while he was imprisoned.

She increased her urgent sucking, and his cock was a dark burgundy color, but it did not yield to her. She orgasmed yet again. She needed control badly. She thought to ask him for it, but this made no sense given their time to date. She thought of sword swallowers in the circus. She fought past her gag reflex. It took a few tries, but she took him down, her nose brushed his tight balls.

Dave grunted, and his limbs went limp as she worked his cock. She loved it desperately, as if the small window she had created would soon be revoked. Tongue, fingers, palms, lips, a touch of teeth, then back down her throat a few times, and he arched his back, lifting her like she was a feather. His voice was silent when the first shot sprayed deep into her gullet, and she nearly lost control of the gag reflex again. She subjugated it. He yelled out. His cock sprayed her mouth. She swallowed him whole again, and he nearly bucked her body off.

She held tight to him like a rodeo champion finishing the bronco ride, still in the saddle.

They lay in a heap, nearly still, totally silent. Only soft, restorative breaths.

The cab was brightly lit. "What the hell did you do to me, Sarah?"

All that came out was, "No bellyache."

He laughed and stroked every inch of her body. She had never felt like this with any man. She had never felt like this at all. She didn't want it to end.

Sarah devoured a big omelet breakfast in the diner. The meal in Reno had burned off halfway across Nevada. She wanted this one to last.

Dave sipped his coffee, nibbled some toast, and didn't try to stop her from paying for both their meals, though clearly he had to fight the reflex. "I'm sure you'll be able to get a ride up to Nampa. I'd sooner take you, but I got a schedule." He started for the cab of his semi. He looked back just once.

"Thanks, Dave." Yes, she was close enough to home that she could get someone to come get her, or thumb a ride north.

She barely heard the words moving away. "I sure will miss you, Little Sarah."

She yelled out. "You never told me where you're headed."

"Next stop, Lincoln, Nebraska. After that, well, lot of roads out there. Still got a bunch to discover."

She walked after him quickly. "Always wanted to see Lincoln." Truly, she never had given it a thought. She grabbed his arm. "You know, it occurs to me we never did work out our differences about Vietnam, Dave."

"You might be surprised what I—" Sarah put her finger tight to his lips. He grinned. "You're right. You got your work cut out for you." He took the suitcase from her hand, walked to the passenger door, and opened it.

She paused for a moment, then smiled and climbed in. "You too, Big Dave." She folded her hands in her lap. He closed the door for her.

# TO BE IN CLOVER

Shanna Germain

Down on his knees in the clover, Dustan wrapped the electric wire around the insulator, pulling it tight. In the field next to him, the wind tickled the corn, making it rustle. The shiver of the tassels sounded like a woman undressing. And when Dustan thought of a woman undressing, he always thought of Maddy.

He cocked his head, listening. There was no wind today. It was bright and still as summer could be, as if the day was holding its breath, waiting. If it wasn't the corn and wind making that sound, then it was Maddy.

In another moment, he could make out the sound of her, the silky-corn swish of her sundress against her legs. He kept at the fence, letting the sound of her come to him in small waves of leg and fabric, and then the smell of her; beneath his own fresh sweat and the sweet waft of the flowering clover came her morning scent. Tomatoes off the vine. Zucchini blossoms. The tang of the marigolds she used for pest control.

She came up behind him and threw her hands over his eyes, and he pretended that she'd surprised him, that he hadn't been anticipating her arrival by sound since she'd entered the field. Her hands were rough with tiny cuts—she never wore gloves—and he reveled in the press of her palms to his eyelids, the momentary loss of light, the way her sounds and smells rose around him to block out the world. Her laughter tickled the edges of his ears.

It was dangerous, the things she did, sometimes. Like blinding him while he was working with fence trimmers and electric wires. But he didn't have the heart to quell her enthusiasm, her childish delight. At least not for his own safety.

She was still laughing when he turned and lifted her a few inches off the ground. She was little but strong, half a foot shorter than him. He settled one hand on her ass, holding her up, loving the way her body filled out there, glorious curves. Not suns. Not moons or melons. Just Maddy and the sweet globes of her ass.

She kissed him, grinding along the front of him as much as she could while he was holding her. Her mouth tasted like raspberries and cream. She wiggled along him, and he had to put her down, out of breath and bending backward. Her bare feet—the toenails painted like mini-suns—disappeared into the clover.

"Maddy, you shouldn't be barefoot out here." He could hear the scolding in his voice, couldn't help it. "You're going to step on a pricker. Or a bee. Or worse."

"I'm fine," she said. "Besides, I'm only interested in being stuck by this particular pricker." He wondered, as he often did, if her daddy knew what a wild creature she was. He doubted it.

Her hand found the front of him, already half-hard, tickling her fingers over his zipper. The flash of her ring in the sunlight as she stroked him, lifting her head, laughing.

"Maddy," he said.

"What?" All innocent, that look, as her gaze caught his—she had deep brown eyes, big and dark, lightly flecked with gold in the centers, and thick dark eyelashes, a sharp contrast to her lighter hair.

On one of their first dates, he'd told her, "You have eyes like a Jersey calf." He hadn't meant to say it—words were his enemy, mostly, things that bit at his tongue and made his cheeks fire. But Maddy hadn't laughed at him; she hadn't gotten angry at being compared to a cow. She'd said, "I don't have to moo when we have sex for the first time, do I?" He'd never thought a woman could say things like that. She said things like that all the time. Words loved her. And he knew then that he wanted to love her like that.

The crazy thing was that she let him do just that. Madeline O'Hara, daughter of Fire Chief O'Hara, Queen of the Country Fair, she of the proper "Please" and "Thank you," she of the gold-brown corn-tassel hair and the calf-brown eyes.

Dustan had seen her his whole life, of course, the way he'd seen all the town girls he'd grown up with. From the outside. Genqua wasn't even that big of a town, but it was big enough to split the farmers and ranchers from the ones who had town jobs, town roles. Maddy O'Hara wasn't just way out of his ballpark. Maddy O'Hara was out of his league.

Except they'd met, officially, for the first time in a ballpark. Dustan playing for the farm team, Maddy's brothers playing for the townies. The farm team had won, and they were heading off for drinks, when this girl in a daisy-yellow sundress and white sandals crossed the field, calling his name.

"Dustan," she said, although everyone else called him Dusty so he didn't know it was his name she was saying until she got close and touched his shoulder.

"Can I go out with the winning team?" she'd asked. The first time he'd seen those eyes, that smile that gave her one dimple on the side, a pushed-in petal.

His teammates were there, standing with him, but he couldn't hear or see them. He could only see the freckles on her chest and the way the sundress cut into her pale shoulders just enough to make red marks.

"I, uh..." His stuttering had been bad then, words more than just an enemy, words a cow kick to the gut that he couldn't step out of the way of.

"Oh, I'll be fine. I'm a big girl," she'd said, as though he'd actually said all of the things that were in his brain. The *what* and the *why* and the way these boys, these farm boys, got drunk and wild beyond what she could have possibly seen, and how the whole other part of him was saying *Please, yes, please.*

"Besides," she'd said, raising her voice in the direction of the other team. "Those town boys are b-o-r-i-n-g."

Later, she said that was their first date, although he hardly counted it. It was beers with the boys and darts. She'd flitted among them like some exotic insect, but one who clearly liked them. And even more clearly liked Dustan.

He still had no idea what she'd seen really in him that day or that night, or the days after, even though she'd told him a million times. "It was that farm-boy muscle in those baseball pants," is what she always said, putting the emphasis on *muscle*. Singular.

She'd let him love her then, and she was still letting him love her now, she was crossing a field of clover and honeybees in her bare feet to bring her pricker-and-honey love to him, to stand on his booted feet and wiggle against him.

"So, you have time for a quickie, Mr. Fence Fixer?" Her words accompanied by her fingers tugging at the bottom of his T-shirt. "Or do I have to go back to the house all sweating and unsatisfied?"

"What, here?" Words came better, without the stutter, but still slow. One or two syllables to her elaborate sentences.

She was nibbling at his neck, laughing. "Mmm, you taste like sweat. And sunshine. More, please."

He meant to resist. He had work to do. The field was flat and open, the clover not even knee high. It wasn't like the time she'd ducked him into the head-high corn, going down on her knees in the mud to suck him. Or the time they'd had sex in the apple orchard, the scent of blossoms and spring grass caught in their hair and skin.

He meant to resist, but she had his shirt up and was running her cool hands along his belly, tucking them into his waistband. "Come down with me," she said. She tugged him down as she went, both of them falling to the ground, the clover a cushion of sweet flower and the quiet buzzing of sun-warmed honeybees.

He remembered his wire cutters at the last second, tossed them sideways out of the way. Maddy cupped the back of his head, brought him down for a giggled, honey-dipped kiss of lips and tongue.

Laughing, they rolled, crushing the clover, bringing him again on top, part of her face covered with the sprigs of green and pink. Looking down at her was pleasure and a kind of pain that squeezed his chest and his cock at once. So beautiful and so his, but in that, the worry of losing her too.

"Fuck me, Dustan." Maddy's eyes up to him, through him. "Please."

And then that thing that always happened, when the giggling stopped and their mouths opened and met, their bodies, still clothed, lined up against each other. As though a switch had been flipped, that electric heat that ran through them both, conducted by desire and pleasure. Dustan felt it everywhere—the tip of his cock, the edges of his lips as they touched hers, his fingertips.

Sometimes he thought his very hair stood on end with the want.

"Gladly," he said. "I've been thinking about fucking you all morning." And, here in that moment, he could talk, fully. He could say all the things in his head without tripping on his tongue, without the words halting him. His face burned when he said things like that, but it burned with a good thing, a safe and yet still dangerous thing. "But I think I'll make you wait...."

Her moan was everything to him, that small sound bitten back behind her lips. He pushed her dress up around her hips, watched the pale skin appear above the carpet of green. She had nothing on underneath, her golden-brown hair trimmed and curled. He dipped a finger, heard the soft groan as she arched her hips toward him, felt his cock harden fully at the feel of her, wet and wanting.

He tucked another finger, marveled as always at the tight, warm pull of her around him. His thumb found the small peak of her clit, circled it lightly until she released another sigh. He could smell her—the sweet arousal from between her legs, the clover crushed beneath her each time she raised and lowered her hips into his hand.

"Please," she said. Her voice was graveled and breath-broken. The one time she had no words, a moment he loved for, lived for. "You're making me...mmm...wait...on purpose."

"I am," he said, leaning down, his fingers still stroking inside her, his other hand pushing the top of her dress down to expose her breasts, taking one small nipple in his mouth, running his tongue in circles that echoed his thumb.

"Dustan..."

Her hands fumbled for his belt. He pulled away at first, content on her, but she kept at it and he let her. It took her two tries, but she finally unhooked the belt and jeans enough so that he could slide out of them.

Maddy tried to sit up—she wanted to suck him, he could tell by the way she moved, by the way she reached for his cock—but he held her there, writhing in the clover.

"Later," he said. "I want to be in you."

She pouted so cute that he almost gave in, but he wanted to feel her warmth around him. Not the active heat of her mouth and tongue, but the way her body rose to his and surrounded him.

He leaned back above her and stroked his cock, once, twice. Who cared if someone saw? That was something Maddy was teaching him every day. The only thing he cared about was the way her gaze followed his movements, the hungry look in her brown eyes, the way she kept saying *Please, please, please*, the sound a wind whisper of want.

She lifted her hips to meet him and he slid into her, slow, teasing, loving the way her body arched, planting her feet to lift her hips and curl her spine upward. Slow, taking his time, watching her, one hand coming between them to tease her clit with each thrust.

Her words totally gone now, just low, moaning breaths, both of her hands gripping his bare ass, pulling him in harder. Her desire made his flare, hot and thick, so that he wanted to plant her into the ground, to plow her under, to go with her into that place where they both bloomed and blossomed.

He slowed his thrusting to lean down and kiss her, trailing his tongue over the edge of her lips and down the curve of her chin. He captured each nipple in turn, sucked hard between his slow strokes.

She caught his head, pulled him up by the hair.

"Stop, stop....stop teasing. Please." Those big eyes, darker with heat, the way the small wrinkles of her forehead came together as she begged. That alone was enough to send him over, never mind the push of her hips against him, the feel of his cock sinking again and again into her depths.

He teased her with his fingers as they fucked, soft and hard on the pressure until she was growling and panting in turn, and then he let his thumb glide across the wet peak, waiting for that moment when she let go, when her body tightened and released and wet his cock with her orgasm.

He didn't have to wait long. He didn't know if he could have. She stuttered his name, once, and then he was rewarded with the intake of her breath that was often the only sound she made when she came. It was all held in her body, the pulled-tight muscles, her eyes shuttered closed and then opened on his face, the nails that found their place in his skin.

And he followed, whispered her name, *Madeline, Madeline,* into her ear. Into her neck. Into the clover and the dirt and the corn next door and the wind that wasn't. And most of all, to all the parts of Maddy that met him and matched him, that took him in fully.

They stayed, tied together with spent desire and the recovering sound of their breaths. He tried to let his forehead rest to hers but ended up thunking her hard enough that they both said *Ow* and then started to laugh.

When he finally rolled away, it seemed like the sun hadn't moved at all, as though they'd stopped time in the middle of the field, in the middle of the day.

A pinprick at the side of his hip; he swore out loud before he realized what it was. A bee or a pricker. From the sting of it, maybe both.

"Aw, baby," she said. She was trying not to laugh as he rolled on his side, both of them eyeing the rising pink welt on his bare hip.

"It was worth it," he said, as he moved back toward her,

letting her head rest in the crook of his arm. The fences could wait. The clover would grow on its own. The bees would do what they did. And the prickers too.

Whatever happened, it was worth it to be here, now, surrounded by the sting and the sweet.

# HONEY CHANGES EVERYTHING

Emerald

Kim wrestled her armload of groceries through the back door and kicked it shut behind her. Setting the bags on the kitchen counter, she glanced at the blinking light on the answering machine and pressed Play.

"Kim, it's Maria. I've been meaning to call you. Drake told me about Terry, and I'm so sorry—we both are. Keep in touch, and if there's anything I can do, please let me know." She paused. Kim could picture Maria's blue eyes shining with sincerity, delicate features emanating concern. "As you may know, Drake's not altogether certain about his job either at this point. Anyway, feel free to give me a call, Kim. Take care."

Kim sighed. She remembered the first time she'd met Maria, the wife of her husband's colleague—former colleague now—Drake, several years ago at the company's annual gala. "Oh my god—your husband looks exactly like Denzel Washington!" had been one of the first things Maria had ever said to her, after their husbands were whisked away for an informal conference

immediately following their introduction. She'd giggled, hiccup-
ping a bit as she turned wide eyes back to Kim. "I hope you
don't mind my saying that."

Kim had laughed. She'd liked Maria immediately, charmed
by the bubbling spunk that seemed somewhat spurred by the
glasses of white wine that occupied the petite woman's hand
most of the evening. She knew what Maria meant, of course,
was that she hoped Kim didn't mind that she had just spent the
last several seconds ogling her husband. Kim didn't mind, and
she'd given Maria a wink as she answered, "I know."

Writing herself a note to call Maria, Kim stuck the Post-it
near the phone and turned to unload the bags on the counter.
It was Tuesday. The news had come a week ago the previous
Friday, when Terry had gone to work as usual with no wisp of
an idea that he would return home a few hours later without a
job. The layoff was a surprise to individual employees, but it
was not surprising in the face of the current economy.

Kim hadn't panicked—it wasn't her style—but the effect it
had on Terry was dramatic. She suspected it was more than
concern about their financial well-being. Losing the job he had
worked so hard at to make his way to second-tier management
hurt something inside him. Something he had taken for granted,
that external circumstances had allowed to be latent. If Kim was
right, though, it wasn't about anything external.

She felt her stomach tighten as she put away the groceries.
The financial implications, of course, would soon make themselves known. They would be okay for this month, and probably
the next. After that was uncertain. Her own catering business,
which she ran from home, had been affected by the economy as
well. Though it had been fairly successful in its three-year life, it
wasn't enough to support them both.

Kim pulled open the refrigerator door, her ebony ringlets

swaying like silent wind chimes in the reflection of its gleaming surface. Catching sight of a smudge as she closed it, she reached for the glass cleaner just as she heard Terry coming down the stairs.

Turning, she saw him enter the living room. She knew he had been upstairs on the computer, most likely searching through jobs or working on his résumé. He shuffled forward onto the linoleum.

"Want some lunch?" she asked.

Terry shook his head, not looking at her as he sorted through the stack of papers beside the phone. Kim watched him, unsure what to say. She couldn't say everything would be okay, because she didn't know that it would. She couldn't tell him not to be scared, because she was too.

She lowered her head with a frown, suspecting again that the demon Terry was wrestling went deeper than those things. Something in him questioned more than the situational concerns, more than what would happen. It wasn't questioning circumstances or emotions or outcomes.

It was questioning him.

Kim set the head of lettuce she had pulled from the refrigerator down and walked over to her husband. He looked up as she fixed her dark eyes on his. Kim almost flinched at the hollow look she saw there, but she straightened herself tall, ready to tell the part of him she knew was saying those things to him to fuck off. She took a deep breath and opened her mouth.

"I love you."

It wasn't at all what she had expected to say, but neither her posture nor her gaze wavered.

Terry's eyes looked dull, though they stayed on hers. "I love you too." His gaze slid away then, back to the papers on the counter in front of him.

Kim let her breath out silently as Terry turned and wandered back to the living room. Reaching to straighten the pile of papers he had been examining, she returned to the counter and picked up the head of lettuce. It felt heavy in her hands.

Thanks to her internal alarm clock, Kim woke up around the time she wanted to on Saturday morning. She glanced at Terry to make sure he was still asleep and eased out of bed, tying her short red satin robe around herself as she padded down the stairs.

Terry had been without a job for three weeks, and his general state seemed even more lackluster than the professional prospects he'd found. Kim was well aware that her husband's résumé was exemplary—highly educated, experienced, and commended, he had demonstrated unquestionable competence and even superiority in his field. The present job market was responsible for the dearth of opportunities, which was the reason he was unemployed in the first place.

She opened the refrigerator and grabbed two eggs, setting them on the spotless counter. All that seemed to have been forgotten by Terry. Whenever she reminded him of either his own competence or the influence of the larger economic environment, it was as though the words dissolved in the air before they ever reached his consciousness.

Smothering a yawn, Kim began to pull mixing bowls and measuring cups from cupboards and drawers as quietly as she could. The counter collected with ingredients as she slid canisters forward from linear rows, the immaculate surface offering itself as her canvas, a steady, solid space upon which to create. She felt the familiar warmth of appreciation for the art of food preparation spread through her body.

Picking up the griddle, she sprayed it with organic safflower oil before setting it on the burner and turning the heat to low. Terry's despondence, which at this point was of more concern to her than financial matters, had been manifesting sometimes as a tightly controlled anger and bitterness and other times as a smothering despair. The night before, when he had left the kitchen after dinner with a whispered, "I'm sorry I've failed us," she had almost thrown a dish against the wall in frustration.

Kim reached for the canister of organic whole wheat flour and wiped away a spot on the side before unscrewing the lid. She reached into the canister, closing her eyes and taking a deep breath as her fingers skimmed over the softness within. She loved the feel of flour. It was one of the ingredients she most loved to touch.

It had been her conscious aim for as long as she could remember to appreciate food preparation with all of her senses. To her, cooking was nowhere near simply a means to an end. It was a transformation, a miraculous process in which elements came together, often in subtly different ways, and yielded a culmination that could be substantially different from what the components had been separately. Every ingredient she used, from olive oil to molasses to a dash of salt, Kim respected as indispensable to the whole she was creating. She took none of them for granted.

Lifting her fingers from the flour, Kim picked up a measuring cup. Her movements were reverent as she measured the ingredient precisely and transferred it to the larger mixing bowl. Then she reached for the organic brown sugar, adding the measured amount to the flour as she licked a few stray grains from her thumb. Baking soda. Two teaspoonfuls landed in white puffs on top of the dry mixture. Finally she grabbed the cinnamon, which went into almost everything she baked, and tapped three brown splotches onto the powdered pile.

Her thoughts returned to her husband as she picked up the eggs. The dispiritedness Terry had displayed since losing his job had included a lack of interest in many things he usually appreciated—including sex. While she didn't take it personally, she suspected the degree to which Terry's subconscious linked his perceived professional success with his sense of personal value was what had made losing his job seem such a staggering blow— and seemed to be threatening his entire self-image. It wouldn't surprise her if a part of him was questioning whether he was still worthy of her affection.

Kim opened the bottle of vanilla and inhaled deeply before tipping it over the bowl. She watched the thick brown ribbon swirl into the pale mixture and screwed the lid back on the small bottle. Frankly, she wasn't interested in rebuilding that self-image back up in Terry. The fact was, he was far more than his professional success, and while she saw nothing wrong with taking pride in them, to her Terry's reaction in the face of losing that perceived source of achievement indicated that it comprised dangerously too much of his appreciation and understanding of himself.

The griddle began to hiss, and Kim lifted the heavy bowl of pancake batter and tipped it until a circle swelled on the sizzling surface. Upturning the bowl, she shifted it a few inches to start the next circle. After repeating the process twice more, she set the bowl back on the counter.

The pale circles glowed like four full moons on the black iron background as Kim began to put the ingredients away, keeping one eye on the griddle. Right after her love of cooking was her love of a clean kitchen. She aimed for her kitchen to be less than immaculate only when she was using it. Ideally, by the time whatever she was cooking was ready, the kitchen was clean again too.

Sparse bubbles began to yawn on the circles of batter like something just waking up. Kim slid the spatula under them and flipped them one by one, the bubbles receding back to the darkness of sleep. She opened a cupboard and reached toward the back. Not feeling what she wanted, she opened it further and peered inside. It took her a moment to remember they were out of syrup.

"Shit," she muttered as she shut the cupboard and tapped her fingers on the counter. She couldn't leave to run out and get some; pancakes were still cooking on the stove. Waking Terry up to do so would defeat the purpose of surprising him with breakfast in bed. She frowned.

Turning back around, she opened the cupboard again. Her eyes went to the thick, solid glass of the honey jar, honeycomb still intact in the center of the golden liquid fresh from the local apiary. Kim considered, then pulled it off the shelf and shut the cupboard door.

Unscrewing the cap, she reached across the counter for the small wooden honey drizzler and lowered it into the jar. Twirling it as she brought it back out, she watched as the barely transparent, lava-like liquid streamed back into its container. When the flow paused, Kim brought the wooden implement to her lips, opening her mouth just as the honey started to fall again. It landed on her tongue, and she moaned quietly. All the more because of its unique, extraordinary, direct-from-nature creation process, honey was one of her favorite foods.

She turned back to the stove and pulled the pancakes from the griddle. Four more full moons were born, and Kim set down the bowl and pulled a plate from the cupboard. She dropped one of the pancakes on it and dipped the honey stick into the jar again. The amber substance spilled back into its own rippled pool as she twirled. During a pause, she moved the stick over the pancake and turned it downward, waiting as gravity slowly pulled the liquid onto the whole wheat disk below it.

Dropping the honey dipper back in the jar, Kim picked up a fork and pulled a bite toward her mouth, feeling the heat from the pancake as it got closer. She stopped short as Terry strode abruptly into view, clad in a pair of gray sweatpants.

"What are you doing?" she said, dismayed that her surprise was spoiled.

Terry rubbed his eyes sleepily. "I woke up and you weren't there. I came down to look for you." He looked behind her to the counter. "What are you doing?"

Kim glanced behind her with disappointment. "I was making you breakfast in bed."

Terry's expression registered surprise. "Oh." A smile formed across his face like the sunrise. "Thank you."

Kim smiled then too, sensing his appreciation of the unfulfilled gesture. She had planned to tell him when she woke him that she wanted to show him that they were still okay, that he was okay, that feeling like a failure didn't mean he wasn't worthy, that he couldn't feel happy, that he didn't deserve to be appreciated—including by himself. Most of all, to show him that she loved him no matter what.

As she watched him, Kim saw that while her carefully executed plan had failed, the intention had been fulfilled. Though she wasn't waking her husband and telling him those things, she could see them transferring to him through the sight of the pancakes bubbling to life on the stove, the warmth of the griddle-heated air, the fragrance of cinnamon and vanilla and whole wheat. She hadn't needed to say a word.

"I forgot we were out of syrup." Kim moved back to the counter and flipped the pancakes on the griddle before lifting the honey jar. "I was just checking to see how they tasted with honey." A drop had fallen onto the counter, a single slip of disorder among meticulousness.

Terry's mouth curved in a smile as he followed her. "A spot on the counter!" he teased, pointing at it. Kim smirked and grabbed a kitchen wipe to clean it up. Terry laughed, and Kim spun around and looked into his eyes. It was a magical sound—one she hadn't heard in weeks.

Her husband pulled the honey jar from her. Kim watched as he lifted the drizzler out slowly, his eyes on the golden liquid as it spiraled back into the pool in the jar. He motioned with his head for her to come closer. Kim started to question, but before she could speak he closed the distance between them himself and untied her robe so swiftly it fell to the ground before she could grab it. He flicked the burner off behind her as he nudged her back against the counter and lifted the honey drizzler to her neck.

Kim started to protest as the amber liquid began to drip, but she froze as it touched her skin. She squirmed as a drop fell to the floor, but Terry pushed on her shoulder, holding her against the counter. She started to speak again, and the words dissipated as he pressed his mouth to the honey flowing over her clavicle. His warm tongue swept over her skin as he claimed the sweet liquid from it.

"Terry," Kim managed to admonish when he pulled away. She gasped as honey landed on her breast—she hadn't noticed his hand moving back to the jar. As she watched, openmouthed, Terry glided the dipper several inches above her chest, drizzling honey in a horizontal line across her breasts.

The sticky liquid began to descend, creeping toward her nipples. Kim opened her mouth to object as Terry dipped his head and caught a nipple between his teeth just as it was engulfed. Her breath caught in her throat, and she remained silent as he grasped her breast from underneath, his tongue swirling over the golden sweetness.

Terry groped her other breast with his other hand, smearing honey across her skin as she let out a muffled moan. He followed it with his mouth, fervently licking the mess he had just made and grabbing the breast his mouth had just left. His mouth and hands became a flurry of action, emphasized all the more by the slowness of the honey as it inched along her skin. Kim lost track of where Terry's hands were and where honey would next land on her body as he lifted her to sit on the counter, his tongue roving her breasts, her nipples, her neck, her throat, her stomach.

She gasped when she felt the distinct sensation of the liquid dropping onto her lower belly and beginning to slide downward. Terry grasped her thighs and pushed them further apart as he hovered, waiting as the honey traveled down her skin. Kim's breath was suspended, barely moving as her cunt pulsed, nothing but the anticipation of Terry's mouth landing there holding any more of her attention. She glanced down to where the liquid shone like glass on her dark skin, moving like a melting glacier toward the heat that awaited it.

The moment the cascade reached her clit, Terry dove. Kim inhaled sharply and dropped her head back, digging her fingers into her husband's hair as he licked and sucked, thoroughly collecting all the honey from her clitoris. To her surprise, Kim felt a climax building as his tongue quivered against her. Orgasm had not usually happened so quickly for her, but now it felt imminent.

Panting, she dropped back on her elbows. Just as the wave was about to come, Terry rose, scooping her off the counter and setting her onto the honey-dotted floor in one swift motion. Kim's resistance to the messiness of the usually impeccable linoleum subsided as his mouth returned to her pussy. He grabbed her ankles and threw them over his shoulders as he squeezed at her tits, his tongue never ceasing its work.

Heat roiled in her like water in a teakettle. When she reached the boiling point she screeched in kind, flailing wildly as the orgasm ravished her honey-drenched body. She rolled in the stickiness, in the utter and inexplicable surrender that made her not just ignore but revel in the messiness, the chaos, the letting go of something she hadn't even known she was holding on to. Her body seemed to sink deeper into the puddles of honey beneath it as Terry's hands gripped her thighs firmly, all traces of the amber liquid long gone from the surface of her clit, still covered by his mouth.

She breathed heavily, opening her eyes, and looked up at her husband. The same embrace of chaos and disorder was reflected in his eyes as he looked back at her.

Uncertainty. Messiness. Surrender. They were part of the recipe. Something had moved, and it went beyond what she had wanted Terry to understand a few hours before when she'd trotted purposefully downstairs in her short crimson robe. Because it had moved in her too. Like the alchemy in cooking, something had been created in the connection greater than and different from the components by themselves.

The kitchen wasn't clean. But it was what it needed to be to have created what was there. Kim tasted honey as Terry kissed her and she wrapped herself around him, their bodies at ease as they lay immersed in the sticky disarray.

# CHEATING TIME

Kate Pearce

By the time Jodi flipped open her cell phone and checked the address, her cab had already driven off down the street, leaving her the option of going into the bar or calling for another ride. She considered the cheap flashing neon sign. Half the letters were already burned out, and the logo now read "mingo." From the fluorescent pink and the dark skeleton of a one-legged bird that perched on the top of the sign, she could only assume the name was supposed to allude more to a tropical paradise than a Californian backwater gold town.

She shuddered as she contemplated the well-kicked-in door. Paradise it wasn't, but she'd already decided she was going through with it. Her date had been very specific about the place she was to meet him, and she didn't want to fuck this up. Time was too precious. Just the thought of seeing him was already making her heart race, and her body tighten in the most intimate of places.

The door was pushed open and a blast of beer-laden air and

the thump of a jukebox hit her in the face. Two guys walked past and gave her the once-over. One of them winked, but she was way too wound up to flirt. She clutched her black purse. Would he care about that? What exactly was he expecting her to do tonight? She should have learned never to make promises when she was drunk.

Doubt clouded her bravado, and she almost turned back. Someone came up behind her and she found herself walking forward into the noisy crush of people enjoying their Saturday night. Immediately she looked around for him, but there were several guys wearing cowboy hats, and some of them even looked like the genuine article with scuffed boots, Wrangler jeans, and faces lined from staring into the sun. The floor was made of wide planks, and despite the sign, the décor was definitely more western than Caribbean.

The jukebox started up, and Jodi had to move to one side to avoid the crush of people who wanted to join the line dancing. She looked down at her open-toe sandals and brand-new red pedicure and winced at the thought of a heavy boot stomping on her delicate toes. But he'd told her what he wanted her to wear, and she'd followed his instructions to the letter. Silky red tank top, short denim skirt, and thong underwear, also red and lacy, and currently damp with anticipation.

She skirted the line dancers and headed toward the bar that was situated against the back wall. The six bar stools covered in cracked black leatherette were all occupied except the one nearest her. Jodi hesitated for a second, and the cowboy sitting closest swung around to stare at her. She almost swallowed her tongue as she recognized her date for the night. His sky-blue eyes were narrowed and focused on her; his smile was slow in coming and full of dark promise.

"There's a seat free here."

"Thanks."

Jodi hopped up onto the stool, hiking her skirt up to accommodate the stiffness of the denim. His gaze settled on her exposed thighs, and she suddenly found it difficult to breathe. Were they supposed to be strangers, then? Was this how he wanted to play it tonight? She gathered her courage.

"Would you like a drink?"

He considered her for a long moment. "You're buying?"

She shrugged and the thin strap of her top fell down her arm. "It's the twenty-first century. We're supposed to be equal now."

"Then I'll have a beer." He caught the eye of the harried bartender straight away and the woman came right over. Jodi held up two fingers. "Two beers please."

"Sure."

She went to open her purse, and he put his hand over hers. The strength and warmth of it shocked her into stillness. "Don't worry about it yet. I've already set up a tab. We can settle up later."

"Actually, I was going to check my cell."

His grip tightened. "Don't you remember our deal? No cell phones and no texting. This is our time."

"Okay," Jodi whispered and waited for him to move away, but instead he picked up her hand and turned it over.

"Nice nails."

"I usually keep them short." Jodi admitted. "But this seemed like a special occasion."

He brought her hand to his mouth and kissed her knuckles. "I like a woman scratching my back and digging her claws in my ass."

"Yeah?" She said weakly. His tongue flicked out, and he licked her index finger and then he sucked it gently into his mouth. Jodi wanted to whimper as her nipples tightened until she knew he'd be able to see them through the silk of her top.

The arrival of the frosted beer bottles made her jump, and he released her hands. She took a hasty swallow and then watched him drink the whole bottle, the regular motion of his tanned throat just adding to her anticipation. He put the empty down and slowly wiped a hand over his mouth.

He gestured at her unfinished beer. "Do you want a glass for that?"

"No, I'm fine with the bottle."

A smile kicked up the corner of his beautiful mouth. "Always a nice sight for a man, seeing a woman's lips locked around the neck of a bottle."

Jodi met his gaze. "And good practice too."

"Yeah," he glanced over at the packed dance floor, where the music had changed to something slower and sultrier. "Would you like to dance?"

"With you?" Jodi couldn't keep the surprise out of her voice.

"Yeah, I can dance."

She felt herself blushing as he held out his hand and helped her off her stool. He stayed close so that her whole body came into contact with his, and he steadied her with his hands at her hips.

The lights were lower now, and he guided her toward the shadows, one hand riding her waist. Jodi reached up and locked her hands around the back of his neck and breathed in the scent of leather and Calvin Klein aftershave. They moved together to the music, her breasts crushed against his checked shirt, her stomach pressed to the hard ridge of his jean-encased erection.

He slid his hands beneath the hem of her skirt and stroked the underside of her ass.

"You wearing those red panties for me?"

"Yes."

"Good." He bit down on her ear and she whimpered. "They won't get in my way then."

His callused thumb moved higher, tracing the lace between her ass cheeks, and Jodi closed her eyes as her knees threatened to give way. He could still do it to her. One touch and she was like warm flowing honey in his hands. The music changed to another slow song, and he bent his head and took possession of her mouth, his tongue thrusting deep as he penetrated her sex with one long finger.

She gasped into his mouth but couldn't escape him, her body way too eager to accept his penetration in any way she could get it. When he finally lifted his head she could only stare up at him in mute appeal. He took her hand and started toward the restrooms.

"Come on."

He didn't stop until they'd exited the back door of the bar and veered to the left. Jodi found herself in a small yard filled with barrels and crates of empty bottles. He backed her up against the nearest wall, his gaze hungry and determined, his hands all over her.

"I can't wait. I want to fuck you right now."

Jodi moaned as he rucked up her skirt to her waist, cupped her ass, and lifted her against the thick wedge of his cock. The denim felt harsh against her swollen wet folds, but she didn't care as he ground himself against her.

"You want this? You want my cock?"

Jodi nodded.

"Then take it out so I can fuck you right here against the wall."

Jodi scrabbled with his metal belt buckle and straining zipper until she revealed his thick shaft. Before she could do more than moan her appreciation, he lifted her and impaled her on his thick heated length. She screamed into his mouth at the sudden penetration, holding tight to his shoulders as he worked himself up inside her in short, sharp, unforgiving strokes.

"Take it, honey. Take my cock in your cunt, make me come."

Jodi concentrated on the thrust and withdrawal of his shaft and the ragged sensations he aroused in her. She anchored her feet on his pumping hips and simply enjoyed the wildness. Had she ever had sex like this before? Probably not since she'd gotten married and certainly not since she'd had kids. She felt his buttocks tighten beneath her heels, and his stroke became shorter and faster as if he was trying to jackhammer his way up inside her.

He managed to shove his hand between them and zeroed in on her clit, thumbing it in hard circles until she started to come around his big cock in an ever-tightening frenzy of need. He groaned into her mouth and climaxed, his cum hot against her clenching, greedy, demanding pussy.

When Jodi opened her eyes, he was still holding her, her legs wrapped around his hips and his cock just inside her.

"We're not done."

Jodi gasped as he started walking toward the parking lot.

"You can put me down!"

"Why?" he kept walking and she felt his cock start to grow again. "I like you exactly where you are."

"But what if someone sees us?"

"I'd like that." He steadied her with one strong arm wrapped around her hips and unlocked the truck. "I'd like them to see me fucking you."

In one fluid motion he opened the passenger door and sat her on the edge of the seat still facing him, his cock growing and pulsing inside her. He was tall enough that he didn't need to join her in the cab, he just widened his stance, grabbed hold of her ass, and started pounding into her again.

"Nice and wet, just how I like you."

When she realized she could plainly see the back door of the bar, Jodi closed her eyes and just hung on, hoping that their current solitude would continue. His teeth closed on her throat, and she stared up at him.

"Stop worrying and concentrate on fucking me. We don't have all night."

That was true. They never had this freedom anymore. Jodi kissed him, drawing on his tongue. His pace increased until all she could hear was the pounding of their hearts and the slick wet sounds of body parts slamming together until her world narrowed to the sensations in her clit and the desperate need to come. He climaxed and she joined him, clinging tightly to his crumpled and damp shirt as he groaned her name.

When he drew away, she whimpered at the sudden loss of his heat. He kissed her nose and rearranged her legs on the seat until she faced forward. He even put her seatbelt on, his mouth lingering over the swell of her breast.

The roar of the truck engine startled her and she stared out into the darkness, a lump forming in her throat.

"Are we done?"

She didn't want to go home to domesticity. She wanted this to last forever.

"Hell, no, we're not done." He glanced at her as he backed out of the parking space. God knows how he'd managed not to lose his cowboy hat, but it was now planted firmly on his head. "Just do something for me before I start driving. Spread your legs wide and rub your clit. I want to make you come straight away when I next get inside you."

She slowly opened her legs, aware that he was watching her,

his narrowed gaze fixed on her wet sex. She touched her clit and gently circled it with the tip of her finger.

"Yeah, that's good." His voice was rougher now. "Now slide your little finger in your ass because you know I'm going to fuck you there before we've finished tonight."

Jodi swirled her smallest finger in the wetness they'd created and tilted her hips forward so that she could ease the tip of her finger inward through the tight pucker of her ass. She imagined his cock there too, much bigger and more demanding, making her beg him to stop, to never stop, to fuck her until she was hoarse from screaming.

The drive hardly seemed to take a minute before he stopped the truck.

"Stay here."

Jodi was quite happy to oblige him. She wasn't sure if she wanted to move ever again. She continued to touch herself until he opened her door and stared down at her.

"Christ," he muttered and bent his head to lick her fingers and clit. She climaxed hard, pushing her sex into his questing tongue. Before she finished coming he picked her up and strode toward a dimly lit building, pausing only to slide the card in the lock and kick the door open with one booted foot. He snapped on the light. The room smelled of dust, bleach, and old carpet but she didn't care. There was a bed and a bathroom, and that was all they'd ever needed.

He laid her carefully on the bed. "I want to see you naked. I never get to see you naked anymore."

She helped him remove her clothes and then he came down over her, his mouth on her breast, one hard thigh between her legs tormenting her already sensitive clit. His fingers slid into her from behind and probed her slick entrance.

"Damn, I wish I had two cocks. I want to fill you up." He

kissed her mouth. "Next time, bring your vibrator with you, okay?"

"Sure." *If there was a next time...*Jodi attacked the snaps on his shirt to reveal every inch of his muscled chest. He didn't need to go to the gym to work out. Life on a ranch was hard enough. She went to unbuckle his belt, and he caught her hand.

"Give me the belt when you've taken it off me. I want to try something new."

Jodi stared up at him, her mouth suddenly dry. She handed him the belt, and before she could start on his jeans, he moved off her.

"Kneel on the bed with your hands behind your back."

She did what he said, her body trembling with a combination of apprehension and excitement. He'd always been adventurous in bed, and she loved every single kinky thing he'd ever shown her.

He wrapped the belt around her wrists and pulled the leather tight through the buckle. "Kneel up." Jodi managed it somehow and he drew the rest of the belt down between her ass cheeks until it was pressed flat against her wet pussy.

He came to stand in front of her, one hand working the zipper of his jeans, the other reaching for the end of the belt. "Suck my cock."

He guided her head toward his shaft, and she took him deep and sucked hard. His hand fisted in her hair, and he rolled his hips in tandem to her sucking.

"That's good, honey." He murmured, his voice turning her on even more. From the corner of her eye, she saw him wrap the end of the belt around his hand. He jerked the leather, sending a jolt of sensation running back along her pussy to her bound wrists. He pulled on the belt again making her moan and writhe against the friction. She wasn't sure whether the sensation was painful or pleasurable, but she didn't care anymore. There was no shame in this. It was all about giving each other what they both so desperately needed.

His hand tightened in her hair. "We're running out of time. Let go of my cock and get on your hands and knees."

Reluctantly Jodi released him, and he helped her turn onto her hands and knees, her wrists still bound with his belt, her ass arched toward him. She shivered as the belt fell away from her sex and at least four of his fingers slid into her pussy.

"Please." She whispered. "Fuck my ass, please."

His laugh was low and desperate. "Do you have lube in that purse? Otherwise it'll just be my cock and it'll be rough."

"I'd take you that way," Jodi said. "You know that, but I do have lube."

He reached for her purse, opened it, and let the contents fall haphazardly onto the bed. "Got it."

Jodi waited in trembling anticipation as he prepared himself and then slid a well-lubed finger into her ass and moved it back and forth. He bent over her, his mouth close to her ear. "I'm a bastard. I like fucking you when you're not completely turned on. I like having to gain every inch and how you can't stop getting all wet around me anyway."

He added another finger and then another, widening her for his cock, and she simply closed her eyes and enjoyed every moment. Sure, she'd be sore tomorrow, but at least she'd have lived a little and escaped her normal boring life. He pulled his fingers out, and she felt the broad head of his cock probe her tight bud. He eased himself inside her, whispering encouragement, sharing every filthy, loving thought he had about how she felt and how hard he was going to fuck her when he was finally inside her.

And he did fuck her—until she was screaming his name and he pinched her clit so hard that she couldn't breathe and couldn't see for the pleasure. After a short while, and a visit to the bathroom, she managed to undress him completely and ride his cock again until he was the one begging and pleading with her never to stop.

She lay sprawled over him, her eyes half-closed, and listened to the steady beat of his heart. The shrill tones of her cell phone had her reaching instinctively for her purse. As she scrabbled to find her cell on the messed-up bed, the screen lit up and Jodi's stomach did a peculiar flip.

Before she could answer the phone, it was plucked from her grasp.

"Why the hell is he calling? Can't we get any peace?"

Jodi tried to grab the cell back, but it was too late.

"What's up, Mikey?"

She tried to understand the excited chatter on the other end of the line, but it was too fast. His face softened and he raised his eyebrows at her.

"Do you want to speak to Mom?"

He handed her the phone and lay back down on the pillows, his expression resigned.

"What's up honey?" Jodi asked.

"The babysitter wants to know if I can play Dark Warriors in Peril. Can you tell her its okay?"

"Is that why you called, Mikey? You're thirteen—you should be able to work this out yourself."

"*Mom*, she says it's for teens only and Darla and Tom aren't old enough."

"Then you get to play it when they've gone to bed. Why aren't they in bed anyway?"

She waited while Mikey conferred in muffled tones with someone else. "They are just going now. When will you and Dad be back?"

Jodi glanced at her husband. "When we're ready."

"Haven't you guys finished celebrating your anniversary yet? Jeez, how long does it take?"

"As long as we want. Fifteen years is a big deal, okay?"

He sighed. "Okay, we'll see you later then."

The phone went dead, and Jodi stared at the now blank screen. She turned to the large naked man stretched out on the bed beside her, and he took her hand.

"I told you to turn that off."

She squeezed his fingers. "I just couldn't."

He sighed, "I know how you feel, but is one night away from the kids a year too much to ask?"

"No, it's not."

Jodi held up her cell so he could see it and turned it off. He deserved this night. *They* deserved it. Having three kids had definitely inhibited their sex life. Perhaps this would help them get back into their sexual groove on the ranch—now that they'd fitted that new lock to their bedroom door.

He smiled and ran a hand down his growing cock. "Then come here and fuck me."

She crawled toward him and bent to lick his already wet crown. "That will be my pleasure."

# OUR OWN PRIVATE CHAMPAGNE ROOM

Rachel Kramer Bussel

I can't believe I'd been married to Derek for two years before I found out about his history in strip clubs. Perhaps that sounds a little too grandiose for what amounts to a handful of visits, but it feels like a secret past that I'd known nothing about, and I am, I'll admit, a little jealous. Maybe more than a little bit. Even though I believe him when he says he hasn't been to one since before we started dating, it's the secrecy that sets me off more than the idea of beautiful, almost-naked women all over him. I'm jealous and turned on and confused by the intersection of the two. Plus it's the present I'm more concerned about than the past, and the fact that I won't be there. He's heading off to his best friend Greg's bachelor party, and suddenly I'm turning into the stereotypical wife, suspicious of what antics these men, and more specifically, my man, might get up to.

But even more than jealousy, what lurks inside me is curiosity. So when Derek tells me that in his single days, when he'd been horny but hard up for dates, he'd spent some of his fancy

Wall Street bonuses in the back rooms, the champagne rooms, of strip clubs, I start to picture what exactly had gone down in those mysterious havens of sexuality. Immediately, I get an image in my mind: my big, strapping man sitting down against a plush leather seat, while a beautiful, petite (except for her breasts) naked girl, glistening with sweat and desire, and maybe some glitter, writhes against him. Sometimes in my fantasies she's bottle-blonde, sometimes brunette like me, but with shiny, glossy, gorgeous hair, sometimes a wild redhead. I can practically see her bare pussy pressing its heat against his thigh, her perfect nipples bouncing in the air while he restrains himself from taking a lick. The more I think about it, the more turned on I am, the momentary flickers of jealousy fading into a throbbing deep inside. I wonder if she teased him, running her finger along his cheek, or maybe his arm, or even, if she were the extra-naughty type, along his cock, knowing he couldn't touch her. That's what I would do if I were in her incredibly tall, probably clear Lucite shoes. The more I think about it, the more I realize I don't just want to see the girl shaking her moneymaker for my man; I want to be that girl in all her hedonistic glory.

I keep these visions to myself, though, because I'm still not quite sure what to make of them. I chat with him nonchalantly, and smile as best I can, but as soon as Derek leaves for his boys' weekend, I'm not sure what to do. Tell a friend? Get wasted? Go to a strip club full of men myself? More than anything, I wish I were there with him, watching him, enjoying his sexy fun by proxy.

Since joining him is not an option, I settle on that last option in my mind, then go into our bathroom, strip, and stare at myself in the full-length mirror. I start to preen, then realize something is missing, and race into my closet to peruse my shoe rack, which is organized by height, from tallest to lowest, stripper shoes to kitten heels. Today definitely calls for stripper shoes, and I select the highest pair, six-inch stunners that I've never worn outdoors. They were sort of a joke when I bought them, but when I slip my naked, thirty-five-year-old feet into them, I'm not laughing. I'm plotting.

Because more than anything, I want to know what it was like for Derek in the champagne room. I want to feel like I'm a part of it, even though that's his past. But isn't the point of marrying someone to merge past with present with future, to become, as best as two people can, one? No, I haven't asked him about every previous relationship, and he hasn't asked me, but I love the way I can be telling a story about something that happened in high school, a decade before I met him, and he'll finish it for me like he was there. He'll remind me of things I'd not only forgotten I'd told him, but just plain forgotten.

So it's not the stripping so much as the being left out that I object to. Sure, we could go to a strip club ourselves, but as much as I keep fixating on the image of a beautiful, naked woman rubbing up against all six feet, 220 pounds of him, I know the fact that she'll surely be younger, thinner, and less jiggly in the ass and thighs than I am will haunt me, and not in a good way. But that doesn't mean I can't do something about it. I reach for the shower radio and tune it to the Top 40 station, and soon I'm dancing with myself in front of the full-length mirror while Britney Spears urges me on.

I look myself up and down, critically but compassionately. I like my long, silky brown hair, shot through at the top with streaks of blonde, and am grateful that I've found the best hairdresser in the world, who can keep it feeling smooth and shiny even when I don't take the best care of it myself. My breasts have always been the feature I'm most proud of, big enough that I need a sports bra when I go jogging but not big enough to look obscene in my tightest sweaters. I've got hips, yes, and a belly, and thighs, and an ass, all of which I'm constantly trying to slim down even though Derek loves to kiss and lick and grab me there. Sometimes he clings to my hips so tightly he leaves bruises, but I don't mind. I have my good days and my bad days when it comes to liking my body, but today is going to be one of the good ones, and tomorrow, when Derek gets home, is going to be one of the best ever.

I hold on to the sink for a moment to make sure I've got my balance, swing my hair down in front of me, then back up, shimmy down as low as I can go, and when I finally reach between my legs, staring deep into my eyes the whole time, I'm soaking wet. I kick off the shoes as the song ends, exhilarated and aroused. I get rid of my clothes and slip into the shower, where I blast the spray as hot as I can stand it, so hot my pale skin will be juicy red. When I shower with Derek, I tone it down, but since he's not here, I go a little wild, and while the spray beats down on my face, I touch myself and picture what I will do, how I will move against him, imagine the noises he'll make when I take the champagne and spray it all over both of us. That image is what makes me come hard, trembling in the shower, and I waste more than a little water simply absorbing that feeling deep into my core. I need it to build me up in case I get nervous when it's time to go for the real thing.

Shopping for liquor has never felt so risqué, but on this trip, while I search for the perfect bottle of champagne, it feels illicit, like I'm cheating somehow. Maybe it's because I didn't give Derek a clue when he called to check up on me that I was planning this. Too much anticipation could spoil it. We rarely surprise each other anymore, even with flowers or naughty notes. It's not that we don't have a great sex life; it's more that we each know exactly what to expect. Even asking for the high-end champagne feels like flirting. I wonder if the clerk sees my nipples harden; I chose a sheer bra rather than a padded one.

I buy two large bottles and a few glass flutes, then bring them home and set them on ice. I strip off all my clothes and walk around the house naked to get in the mood. I have no idea if real strippers like to be au natural or not, but I know for me it takes a little getting used to. Even when we're on vacation, at resorts where everyone is letting it all hang out, I still cling not just to my bathing suit but a cover-up too. Even a sheer one is better than nothing. But this time I have a little Britney Spears, a little Christina Aguilera, and a lot of courage racing through my blood. I don't plan to drink the champagne myself; that would defeat my purpose if I used it to spur me on.

The champagne is for Derek to enjoy...when I pour it all over myself. I get through a few Britney tracks, a few Christina, a little Rihanna, shaking my ass, my hair, my breasts, every part of me. I do it barefoot and in heels, and I get used to bending over, flashing myself, running my hands over my body. I'm flushed and filled with a new kind of sexual energy by the time I'm done. I slip into the deep peach silky nightie and start to curl my hair. Even though I plan to shake it all over, I have an hour to kill and want to make sure I look stunning for him. I want to make sure Derek knows how much I want him, not just tonight, but always, how much I'd do for him, with him, to him.

The curling iron heats up quickly, and in only a few minutes my hair looks elegant. I pin some of it up and let the warm curls fall around my neck. Normally I'm a lip gloss and maybe dash of blush kind of girl; my weekly manicures and pedicures are my big concession to glamour. But that doesn't mean I haven't raided Sephora a few times, and I discover a treasure trove of barely used makeup. Though I don't wear it often, I didn't grow up with two older sisters and walk away not knowing how to do a perfect smoky eye. I layer on the liquid liner, then a glittery purple shadow, then add false eyelashes I've been saving for a special occasion. This damn well better qualify.

I lotion myself up then prance around the house in my favorite heels as I try not to touch myself again. That would deprive Derek of the sex-starved, nympho side of me. When I hear his keys jingling in the door, I compose myself. I'm the good wife gone bad, and a quick glance in the hallway mirror confirms I look the part. He starts to say, "I'm home," but stops at "I'm" when I walk toward him and give him a big hug. Is it me, or does he look even hotter than when he left?

"Honey, I..." He just stands there with his jaw open, unable to say anything else.

"How was the bachelor party?" I ask.

"It was fun," he says with a cautious note in his voice as he looks around. "Am I...interrupting something?"

I realize he thinks he's walked in on me in the midst of some clandestine affair. He has, in a way, but not in the way he thinks. "No, you're right on time. The show's about to start," I purr, running my hand up his chest.

"Show...?" he asks in a bewildered voice, but I tug him up the stairs, facing him and walking backward, ensuring that he'll want to follow me. Derek is still staring at me like he's not quite sure where his wife has gone, but when I suck on one of my manicured fingers, then trace that finger over my nipple, letting it pebble against my nightie, all while I hold on to the banister with my other hand and take slow, deliberate steps upward in my heels, I know I have his attention. I can make out that he's hard, but even more than the erection I can see, I like the sense of adventure I can taste in the air between us, something that's been missing for far too long.

I've dragged our favorite giant plush chair, the one I know will hold both of us because I've sat in his lap on it plenty of times, from the guest room into our room, and I pull Derek inside and plop him down there. "Sit back, relax, and enjoy the show. No touching though; you might get kicked out. I can touch you if I want to though," I say in a sex-kitten voice I'm not sure I've ever used with him or anyone. It seems to come out of me, or rather, Ginger, the girl I'm channeling, the one I imagine has danced for my husband dozens of times. I start up the playlist I've created, saving the champagne for later. "Closer" by Nine Inch Nails starts to boom through our elegant bedroom, and I can only hope the loud rock takes him to a slightly more edgy headspace. I lift my leg and place the sole of my five-inch shoe on the edge of the chair.

Derek swallows hard. "Sar—," he tries to say, but I silence him with a finger over my lips. I flash him my bare pussy, then flip the nightie down, put my leg down and turn around. I dance for him, for me, for us. I dance for all the times before I met him when I wish I'd been with him rather than with everyone who came before him. I dance for Trent Reznor, pouring every ounce of myself into the song. Keeping with the theme, "I'm a Slave 4 U" by Britney comes on, and I grab the little purple suede flogger I bought yesterday and whip it all around. I stroke it over my breasts and lash it against my arm. I hold out his palm and strike it against him, smiling as he moans. I slap it against my ass, but when Derek reaches to touch me, I push his hands away. Britney might be a slave for someone, but I'm in charge right now.

As the song ends, I toss the flogger on the floor and climb up onto the chair with him, pressing my bare sex directly against him, designer pants be damned. I breathe against his neck, purr into his ear, lick the stubble along his cheek. I sacrifice the nightie and rip the delicate lace at the top so my breasts can spill out as

Madonna launches into "Justify My Love." That's not exactly what I'm doing right now; I'm not justifying it, I don't think, I'm exploring it. I'm telling him that he doesn't have to hide anything from me. I placed my hand on his forehead and stroke downward, and when I lift it, his eyes are closed. That's when I slide my hand under the bed and unearth the giant Veuve Clicquot Brut Yellow Label bottle I've chilled in our freezer. I bring it toward him and hold the frosty glass against his wrist.

Derek's so-beautiful-I-want-to-melt-into-them hazel eyes flutter open and he stares at me with a look that I think means, "You're crazy, woman, but I want to fuck you so badly." I pop the top and pull out the cork, watching the steam rise and hiss its way into the air and then the bubbles exploding upward out of the bottle's mouth. Neither of us can miss the sexual overtones of that. Then I look up at him before leaning down and, in another nod to Madonna, wrap my lips around the bottle. I use both hands to raise it, then swallow a little, letting most of it dribble down my chest, wetting what's left of my nightie, slithering down past my pussy, onto him. I toss my head back, my hair spilling down my back, then pour the chilly liquid directly down my front.

I put down the bottle and again climb up next to my husband, straddling him, and offer him a champagne-soaked nipple. He greedily takes it in his mouth. I reach for his hands and place them on my ass. He grabs me like he hasn't grabbed me in years. His lips, his hands, his cock pressing up against me, are all reminders of what I want us to be like again. The fire didn't exactly go out, but it has fizzled, and only when I hear the roar release from his lips, then feel Derek tearing my nightie right down the middle, do I realize exactly how much I've missed it.

He doesn't say anything, doesn't try to reassure me with words. Instead he lifts me up, my legs wrapped around him, the wet filmy fabric clinging to me. He doesn't bring me to the bed, but instead slams me up against the wall. He keeps me pinned there while undoing his pants. "Is this what you want, Sarah? You want me right here, like this?"

"Yes, yes, yes," I cry when he shifts me just so and places the tip of his cock inside me. He is lighting the spark that is making our relationship explode, making it crackle and sizzle and burn the way it should have been all along. I know as he plunges inside me, holding me tight, his face buried in my neck, that no matter what happened in those champagne rooms, it was never like this. Derek pounds into me, overtaking me, and I cling to him, my thighs straining, my nails digging into his back.

He is fucking me, that's the only way to describe this, yet in its way, his fucking is lovemaking too. It's the kind of fucking a couple can engage in who knows that there is no one else they'd rather be with, so they can slam and rock and thrust and claw, scream and pound and yell and bite, and be assured that the other person wants every ounce of ferocious, almost violent energy they have to share. He doesn't say anything, not even my name, just growls into my ear, a sound that's so beautiful I start to cry a little when I come. He used to tell me not to cry, but now he knows that when it happens, it means I'm so overwhelmed with not just love and lust but destiny, rightness, perfection, that I can do nothing else. I squeeze him hard, and then I come again when he starts to fill me with his passion. He stops thrusting and simply lets himself be inside me, making me his and telling me he's mine.

Only later, when we're freshly scrubbed from a dual shower, and I've remembered the champagne flutes and filled one for him, does Derek dare ask me what was going on before. "Well, the champagne room thing...it made me curious. And a little jealous. I was picturing you with all these girls around you doing all sorts of things and I wanted to, I don't know, recreate that or something."

I mumble the last bit into my pillow. "Baby, you know you're the hottest woman I've ever laid eyes on. And trust me...nothing even close to what you just did ever happened in any champagne room I've been in. But you don't have to show off for me, unless you want to." He looks deep into my eyes and I smile at him.

"What if I want to? I mean, I did buy two bottles of champagne...."

"I say tell me where to install the stripper pole." He laughs but sees my raised eyebrow. "I've created a monster, haven't I?" he asks.

I straddle him, then suck his lower lip in response. I'll show him a monster, all right—a sex monster! And that's exactly what I do for the rest of the night.

# TILL THE STORM BREAKS

Erobintica

Shrimp cocktail glasses filled with Veuve Clicquot. Boxed macaroni and cheese served in plastic bowls. Jars of storm candles for illumination. Pillows and blankets spread on the floor in front of the woodstove. Snow pelting the windows. Not exactly how we'd planned to celebrate the arrival of the New Year.

My friend Teresa was looking in the cabinet for some glasses. "Wow, listen to that wind howl. I'm surprised we still have power. Ah, here's some appropriate stemware!" She'd found some glasses that had, at some point in the distant past, held tiny shrimp in bland cocktail sauce. "The fine crystal!" Her mood was chipper despite our predicament. Of course her optimistic outlook is one of the reasons I'd invited her along. She's fun to be around, and right now, I needed some fun more than anything.

I stood at the stove, stirring occasionally, keeping watch so the macaroni didn't boil over. This wasn't what I'd wanted to be doing tonight. I should be all gussied up in my new red dress and partying till dawn at the fancy beach house my filthy rich, bachelor brother-in-law Greg owns, dining on lobster and gourmet Whoopie pies. At least we had the good champagne that Teresa had insisted on bringing.

This was all my idea, this trip. A real step outside of my comfort zone. Our comfort zone. Every year Greg invited Tim and me to come to his place for New Year's Eve, and every year we found some reason not to go. Or I should say, Tim found a reason. He was never really clear on why he didn't want to. I suspected some sort of sibling rivalry, since Greg lived in a $2 million architect-designed creation overlooking the ocean, and we just had a dull, suburban condo.

Oh, and this little lake cabin, which had been in Tim's family for decades. It wasn't anything fancy; it didn't even really have any character. Very utilitarian. The downstairs consisted of one large room with a small kitchen in one corner and a woodstove in the other. A sofa bed, coffee table along one wall, and a small round table for eating at along the other. Under the stairs to the loft was a bathroom with a stall shower. The loft was open to below and was basically just a floor. We used an inflatable mattress when we stayed up there.

So most New Year's we'd stay home, or maybe go out with some of his office buddies and their wives, a boring crowd if there ever was one. I was tired of it. I'd hit my forties, our daughter was at college, my job was dull, and I was ready for something. But what kind of something? This year I accepted Greg's invitation before Tim had a chance to come up with an excuse. He'd been a little perturbed, and then doubly perturbed when I told him I was inviting Teresa. "Don't tell me you're trying to set Greg up with her. You're not, are you?"

It actually hadn't occurred to me. Yeah, Greg was unmarried, by choice he'd said, and seemed to have a steady stream of attractive women to spend time with. He didn't seem like he needed any help. And Teresa was newly divorced and "not on the market," as she so aptly put it. I'd met her at a weekend writer's retreat, and we'd discovered we lived practically next door to each other, in neighboring towns. She'd just moved there after her divorce, which was why our paths had never crossed before. It turned out she was several years old than me, but she seemed much more vivacious, and her attitude rubbed off on me when we spent time together. I guess Tim likes her well enough. He's fairly set in his ways and always seems amused at my tendency to want to try new things. I love him to pieces, but I guess I'm feeling sort of blah about our relationship.

Tim stoked the woodstove and mumbled something about wishing we'd have hit the road sooner. A couple of days ago, when we'd arrived here on the lake, a stopover on the way to Greg's, the forecast was for a chance of snow on New Year's Eve. There were only a couple of inches on the ground, and the lake had only begun to freeze over. The chance of snow became a storm watch, then a warning, and finally a blizzard warning.

Tim called his brother to tell him we wouldn't make it, then spent most of the day preparing for the storm. Bringing in firewood, filling water jugs, making sure the snow blower had gas, running to the mini-mart and getting some food. White cheddar mac, chips and salsa, a quart of milk, a package of donuts, and a couple of cellophane-wrapped Whoopie pies that were on the counter next to the cash register. We were set.

I tested a noodle. Not quite ready. I watched the bubbles rise to the surface and pop. Best laid plans. Best plans to get laid. I'd been looking forward to the guest suite that I knew Greg would have put Tim and me in, the one with the Jacuzzi and the floor-to-ceiling windows looking out at the ocean. I'd fantasized about Tim unzipping my red dress while I watched our reflection in the window. I loved to have sex when we were away from home. Hotel rooms with their double beds. Quaint bed-and-breakfasts with quilts on brass beds. On the floor at his parents' house, since they'd never replaced the boys' bunk beds. Tent camping. And here at our cabin. But not this time.

We were sleeping in the open loft, and Teresa was on the pull-out. While I might have slid my hand into his pajamas, trying to interest him in something other than sleep, I knew that with Teresa so close downstairs that Tim would just not go for it. He was a pretty vanilla guy and not very forthcoming when it came to sharing fantasies or out-of-the-ordinary desires. But I loved him, and he seemed to enjoy my efforts to spice things up a bit. I realized as I stood there that I was just a little bit aroused. That's what I get for thinking about sex, which I did on a regular basis.

"Hey, are the noodles ready?" Teresa looked over my shoulder. I stabbed one of the macaronis, held it up and blew on it, then fed it to her. "Done?"

She smiled and nodded, and I watched her red hair sway with the movement. I felt an odd little rush as I became acutely aware of her breasts pressed against the back of my arm. Not wanting to move, yet needing to drain the noodles, I turned off the stove and emptied the pan into the colander in the sink. Steam rose, fogging the window. Just then the lights blinked.

"Uh oh," Teresa said, "maybe we should light one of those candles in case..."

We were plunged into darkness. Tim had his flashlight out right away, and I found the matches and started to light the jarred candles we'd placed around earlier. The cabin was soon filled with a soft glow. Glad that I'd gotten the noodles cooked before the power went out, I added the butter and milk and tore open the packet of neon cheese powder. Wow. Special. I grabbed the plastic bowls and forks and put them on the table along with the pan of mac and cheese.

"Dig in."

There must have been something in the tone of my voice that made it obvious I was not happy with this turn of events, because Teresa announced, "Time to open the first bottle of champagne! I think our chef needs a glass!" She draped a dish towel over the bottle, quietly popped the cork, and poured the elixir into the curvy glasses.

"A toast! To the winter storm, friends, macaroni and cheese, and champagne!"

We laughed and proceeded to feast while Teresa kept our glasses filled. Soon I didn't mind the raging blizzard outside at all. Somehow the talk turned to sex, and I felt just like I did back in college when my roommate and I talked in hushed tones about blow jobs and such. Excited and not just a little embarrassed. When the second bottle of bubbly was uncorked, we moved closer to the woodstove. I spread one of the extra blankets on the floor, not sure why, but the carpet seemed cold and I was wanting cozy. As I tossed pillows from the sofa around the blanket, Teresa brought the bottle and the Whoopie pies over.

For awhile we sat quietly sipping, aware there'd been a transition in mood as well as location. Teresa was the one to break the silence, of course, and she broke it with a sledgehammer.

"Have you guys ever had sex with someone else?"

I was dumbfounded, and for some reason first focused on the fact that Teresa always said "guys" even when she was referring to a group of all women. I wasn't sure why she was asking, since she and I had talked a little about what our sex lives had been like before we'd gotten married.

Tim stuttered out, "Well, of course we weren't the first for each other."

"No, I mean have the two of you together ever had sex with someone else? You know. A threesome."

I decided that we must all be officially drunk now. Tim's mouth was literally hanging open in that cartoon kinda way with his glass paused in midair. Oh great, I thought, he had been a good sport up to now, but I knew he was uncomfortable talking about sex and knew I'd hear about it later.

But when he finally answered, I heard something new in his voice, and I watched in astonishment as he said, "No, we haven't, not yet. Are you offering?"

Was I hearing correctly? Had I had too much champagne? Had he? That's when I saw Teresa looking at me intently, and I remembered how I felt when she stood at my shoulder by the stove. Oh shit. She was serious!

Teresa laughed and poured us more champagne and unwrapped the Whoopie pies. I was glad of the chocolate cake and sticky sweet filling to distract us for awhile but couldn't help but notice my arousal. I kept stealing glances at her, noticing her body as if for the first time. It's not like I've never thought about being with a woman, but it was always in the abstract. I've never actually contemplated touching a woman's body in a sexual way, and I couldn't stop thinking about it now.

I glanced at Tim, just as Teresa held a piece of cake out to him, and watched my husband take the cake in his mouth. It was like slow motion: his lips closing over her fingertips, his eyes on her face, her smile as she slowly withdrew from his mouth. I kept waiting to be angry, to be jealous, to want to send them both out in the storm. But all I felt was a rush between my legs, my heart pounding, and my breath coming in short quick inhalations. I was so turned on it wasn't even funny. Right then I knew what I wanted to do. I'd never done it before, didn't even quite know how, but I wanted us all to fuck. Fuck all night long. Fuck till the storm broke.

Teresa looked at me with an obvious question in her eyes.

Could she?

I nodded and tilted my head at Tim. "Go ahead, I want to watch for awhile."

I was startled at my own words. Even when by myself I'd always had to look at porn a sideways manner. Nope, I'm not *really* watching this. But that damn phone better not ring! Now, there I was, watching it live. And even though they'd only just started kissing, I was already soaking through my pants.

He reached out and cupped her breast, rubbed his palm on her nipple. She arched and sighed, running her hands up and down his cross-legged thighs. I knew his cock must be straining against his jeans. I wanted to touch it. I wanted her to touch it. She kissed his neck, kissed the stubble he hadn't shaved off that morning. My lips knew what her lips were feeling as they traced his throat. I wanted to know her lips.

A little unsteadily, I crawled to them. The champagne had definitely had the proper effect, and I giggled as I reached them. Teresa smiled and reached for my hair. Straight, brown, and unremarkable hair, but as soon as she wrapped her fingers in it, I felt incredibly sexy. She pulled me toward her, and our lips met. I wanted to put everything on pause so I could study this new texture, concentrate on the different taste. But her tongue was in my mouth and her hand on my breast, and I could not think anymore. I felt another hand, Tim's, on the other breast, and I reached for each of them. Literally shivering with desire, I opened my eyes and gazed at Tim. Saw the lust in his eyes. And not just lust for Teresa, but lust for me, something I'd not seen in awhile.

The pause was just long enough, and then we tossed pillows aside and tumbled together, kissing and caressing with abandon. Hands were everywhere, and when, unspoken, we reached the point of removing clothes, Tim threw a couple more logs into the woodstove to help keep us warm. I pulled my sweater over my head and felt lips, his, kiss a nipple while her hand gave my other nipple a slight pinch. Gasping, I threw my sweater over toward the sofa and reached to pull off Tim's shirt. Then I took Teresa's hand and placed it on Tim's crotch. I wanted her to unzip his jeans, free his cock, and I wanted to kiss her as she wrapped her hand around his stiffness. I watched as Tim undressed her, watched his cock twitch at the sight of her shaved pussy. I've kept all my hair, and soon he is comparing, fingering each of us.

A brief question of "*Does he prefer her bareness to my bush?*" floated through my head, but as I felt him tangle his fingers and give a tug as he lowered his mouth to my cunt, any worries evaporated. Teresa watched him and ran her own fingers through her folds, slick and shiny wet even in the soft, flickering glow. I reached out and placed a hand on her thigh, pulled her toward me so I could rest my head in her lap. My fingers gently explored her, female but other. Her smell was different from mine, though I couldn't describe it. Slowly, I pushed my tongue into the incredible softness that was her. Was that what it was like to taste me?

Tim stopped to watch me lick Teresa's delicious vulva. I played with her labia, folding the lips back on themselves, then pinching them together gently. She moaned and began to grind against my hand. I slipped a finger inside her, thinking it would feel like when I slip a finger inside me, but it didn't. I was surprised and pleased, and even more aroused. I added more fingers and stroked her, pressed against that fleshy spot that makes me gasp. Tim moved closer and soon his hand joined mine. Together we were finger-fucking her, and she was bucking against us. I hadn't felt this close to him in a long time.

"Fuck her," I said to him, almost breathless. "I want to see your cock slide inside her. I want to watch, and I want my fingers in her too when she comes."

Where was all this coming from? I only wondered for a split-second before his cock disappeared inside her juicy cunt and she was moaning in a voice too real to be a pretend porn voice. My cunt needed something, and I shoved fingers inside myself and humped my hand while I watched my husband madly fuck my friend. My brain fast-forwarded through all I wanted to do, and soon I was coming, crying out and slumping over.

Teresa whispered frantically to me, "Your hand, put your hand down there."

I knew what she wanted. I moved slightly behind Tim's pumping body and slid my hand down, over his balls, to where his cock joined her cunt. I pressed my hand there, feeling them both as they came, feeling the pulsations and flooding wetness.

We stayed in a heap for a bit, catching our breath. The fire had died down, and our sweaty bodies chilled quickly. We untangled. Teresa pulled the blanket up and wrapped it around me and then her. Tim grabbed some more wood and fed the stove, then joined us.

"Wow." That's all I could say. How fuckingly eloquent. Then I giggled.

Tim smiled and leaned in to kiss me. "I love you so much. I've never told you before about this being a fantasy of mine, being with two women. I was afraid to. But this was incredible. Thank you."

Teresa was smiling. "You guys are so lucky to have each other. And I'm lucky to be here with you!" Outside the blizzard was still raging. "It's not even midnight! Who wants more champagne?"

# THE CURVE OF HER BELLY

Kristina Wright

Brynn was crying. Again.

As Paul closed the front door behind him and heard the sobs coming from the bathroom, he felt a thread of frustration winding its way around a ball of empathy. When they had decided to try to get pregnant, Brynn had been thrilled—she was a freelance copywriter who worked from home and couldn't wait to become a mother. At least she had been thrilled, until about eight weeks into the pregnancy, when she started throwing up morning, noon, and night.

Now, seven months pregnant and feeling like there was no end in sight, Brynn cried at the drop of a hat. Anything could set her off—a vitamin commercial, the grocery store being sold out of her favorite juice, a cute puppy loping along the boardwalk— and Paul had learned to tread on eggshells lest he be accused of being insensitive. It wasn't that at all, he kept telling Brynn. It was just that he didn't know what to do to make things better. And that, more than anything, was the root of his frustration.

Bolstering every ounce of patience he could muster at six o'clock on a Monday evening, Paul walked down the hall and tapped lightly on the closed bathroom door. "You okay, baby?"

"No, I'm ugly!"

Paul sighed and bumped his head against the door. "Can I come in?"

The sound of splashing and then, "I guess."

He opened the door and caught his breath. Brynn was in the bathtub, her long blond hair twisted up in a knot on her head, a pouf of bubbles surrounding her pale, naked body. The only illumination was the fading sunlight through the bathroom window above the tub, and Brynn seemed to glow in that golden light. If not for her red-rimmed eyes and shiny red nose, she would look like a mermaid splashing about in the tub. A sexy mermaid. Paul felt something inside him catch—and he smiled gently. He loved this woman, no matter how crazy she made him sometimes. Loved her and wanted her.

"The water isn't too hot," Brynn said quickly. They had been reading the baby books in bed together before they went to sleep—about the only thing they really did in bed anymore.

"I'm sure it's fine."

Brynn sunk down lower in the tub, the peak of her pregnant belly remaining above the surface of the water. "Don't look at me, I'm hideous."

Paul perched on the edge of the tub, studying her. "No, you're not. You're stunning."

Shaking her head stubbornly, Brynn pointed to her stomach. "I found a stretch mark. All these months of slathering myself with cocoa butter and my skin is bursting anyway."

"Where? I don't see anything."

Brynn pointed to a faint purple mark that started an inch

or so under her belly button and disappeared into the water. *There*. It's ugly. These things are like gray hairs—where there's one, there will be more. I'll be covered in them."

A fresh bout of tears followed, and Paul couldn't help but chuckle.

"Why are you laughing at me?" Brynn sat up, more indignant than modest. "It's not funny. I look like a whale."

"You look like a mermaid."

"Don't try placating me," Brynn accused. "I know what I look like."

Paul slipped to his knees beside the tub, the water that had splashed over the side of the tub soaking through his trousers. "No, you don't know what you look like. You're emotional and afraid and you look in the mirror and see how your body has changed and think it's a bad thing—but it's not."

He took Brynn's face in his hands. "Listen to me. You are beautiful. I love the way your body is changing."

To prove his point, he moved his hand from Brynn's cheek down to her full, dark-tipped breasts. They were exotic, earthy—larger than he'd ever seen them. Paul felt something he hadn't allowed himself to feel in months out of respect for Brynn's self-consciousness and discomfort: desire. Hot and needy desire. Without thinking, he cupped Brynn's breasts in his hands. He thumbed the distended nipples and watched them tighten under his firm caress.

"What are you doing?" Brynn asked, a tremor in her voice.

Paul looked into those dark cerulean eyes, so suitable for a sexy mermaid. "I'm showing you how beautiful you are."

Brynn squirmed under Paul's touch, her eyes wide. "That feels...nice."

Paul grasped her nipples between his thumb and index fingers and gave them a gentle tug. "Yeah? You like that, baby?"

Brynn nodded, her nostrils flaring. Tendrils of blond hair escaped their confines to curl around her face. She looked innocent and wanton at the same time.

Paul moved his hands lower, following the contours of Brynn's growing belly. It was round and taut, and he felt the baby kick beneath his touch. They both laughed at that, but this wasn't about the baby. Paul slipped his hand between Brynn's legs, lightly stroking her blond pubic curls.

"Stop. I hate all that stupid hair," Brynn said.

Paul ignored her and kept stroking her. Before the pregnancy, Brynn had waxed her pubic hair so that she was bare and smooth, but her skin was too sensitive for that now. Paul liked the silky-springy feel of the hair beneath his fingers, and he tugged lightly, watching Brynn's face as she did. Brynn's eyes went wide, and she caught her breath.

"That's a strange feeling," she said.

"Good?"

Brynn nodded. "Yeah, I think so. Tingly."

Paul smiled. He slipped a finger between the lips of Brynn's pussy and found her clit. He was rewarded by Brynn's audible gasp. Paul didn't go further than that; he simply rested his finger on that sensitive button as he cupped her mound lightly.

Staring into Brynn's eyes, Paul could see the war Brynn fought with herself. Uncomfortable in her own skin, she hadn't let Paul touch her like this in months. Paul longed to make love to her, but he wouldn't push her. He would let Brynn decide.

Brynn didn't say a word. She didn't have to. She sunk down in the lukewarm water and covered Paul's hand with her own. She pressed his finger hard against her pussy, letting out a soft moan when Paul took the lead and rubbed her clit.

It was something so simple—hardly the stuff of an earth-shaking sexual experience—but Brynn's acquiescence sent a rush of heat through Paul. He wanted Brynn. Now. He wanted to fuck her the way he had before they'd gotten pregnant. He wanted to feel Brynn's body grinding against his, both of them slick with sweat and so aroused they couldn't get enough of each other.

He pressed a finger just inside Brynn's pussy, feeling the heat and wetness there, so different from the tepid bath water. Brynn gasped, gripping Paul's wrist tightly and wriggling beneath his touch until water splashed over the side of the bathtub.

"Easy, baby," Paul soothed. "I'll give you what you want."

Brynn looked at him, blue eyes heavy-lidded with lust, her expression one of complete trust. "I know you will."

Paul slid his finger deeper, feeling Brynn's muscles reflexively tighten around her. "Been practicing your Kegels, I see," he said.

Brynn giggled and nodded. "Yeah."

"Good girl." Paul slipped another finger inside her wetness, curving them up and forward to rub that rough spot he knew so well. "How's that?"

"Oh!" Brynn exclaimed, sloshing water over the edge of the tub as she took Paul's fingers inside her. "Yesssss!"

Paul's clothes were soaking wet at this point, but he didn't care. All he cared about was making Brynn feel good. He twisted his fingers inside Brynn's pussy, feeling the slick wetness of arousal. It fueled his own desire, coaxing his passion beyond gentleness. He tweaked one of Brynn's nipples between his fingers, delighting in the damp, rubbery texture of the skin beneath his touch.

"You're so fucking sexy," he said, barely recognizing his own voice.

Brynn cupped her full breasts, head thrown back against the side of the tub. "Fuck me with your fingers," she whispered. "I need to come."

Her words drove Paul to the edge. He added a third finger

inside Brynn's swollen pussy, filling her. He laced his fingers together and made a twisting motion as Brynn's muscles clenched down on him. He didn't want to be gentle anymore, wasn't even sure that he could. He just wanted to fuck Brynn—hard. He looked into Brynn's half-closed eyes, searching for approval.

"Are you sure you can take this?"

Brynn nodded. "Oh yeah. I want it. Do it."

That was all the encouragement Paul needed. Oblivious to everything but the feel of Brynn's pussy clamped around his fingers, he began to fuck her hard. Water sloshed every which way, causing a tidal wave in the bathroom until the floor was soaked and Brynn was only half-covered by water. Paul braced his right hand lightly on Brynn's wet, swollen belly as he finger-fucked her with his left hand. It was like fucking a beautiful, familiar stranger—and that aroused him in a way he could never have predicted.

"You're so wet, baby," he growled, pushing his fingers deep inside Brynn.

Slowly, so slowly Brynn closed her eyes and whimpered with the anticipation, Paul drew his fingers out again. He could feel Brynn's pussy ripple against his fingers, trying to hold them inside, trying to get off. Paul pushed his fingers back inside Brynn, stroking her swollen clit with his thumb. Brynn nearly came out of the bathtub at that, shrieking as she gripped the edge of tub.

"I guess you like that," Paul muttered, doing it again.

"You're driving me crazy."

With his fingers buried inside Brynn's wetness, Paul kept rubbing his thumb against her clit. "I know the feeling. Know what I want, baby?"

Brynn's eyes fluttered opened and she tried to focus on Paul's face. "Hmm?"

Paul stilled his thumb on her clit. "I want you to tell me you're beautiful."

Brynn jerked against him. "What?"

"Tell me you're beautiful," Paul repeated, emphasizing his words with a wiggle of his fingers. "Tell me how beautiful you are."

Brynn stared at him, as if he'd asked for something perverse. "Don't tease me like that," she whispered.

Paul stroked her pussy again, building a back-and-forth rhythm inside Brynn that caused a wave to lap up against the swell of Brynn's rounded belly.

"Oh, the water feels good," Brynn moaned, rocking against Paul's hand so the water sloshed over her again.

"Tell me," Paul repeated. "You're beautiful. Tell me and I'll make you come so hard, baby."

Brynn whimpered again, eyes closed and head thrown back. She was close to orgasm, Paul could tell by the way her pussy tightened on his fingers. He kept finger-fucking her, driving his fingers deep into her, reveling in the way Brynn's body held him inside.

"You're beautiful, baby," he said. "Beautiful and fucking sexy and I can't wait to get you out of that tub and spread you across the bed so I can make you come again and again."

His litany of words aroused him as much as they were intended to arouse Brynn. His cock ached to be touched, licked, sucked, and enveloped by Brynn's sweet pussy, but this was about Brynn and making her feel good. Making her feel as beautiful as she looked.

Paul stilled his fingers once again. "Tell me, baby. You know you're beautiful, all soft and round and fuckable. Tell me."

"Please," Brynn moaned. "Make me come."

Paul gently rubbed Brynn's G-spot, feeling the swollen, spongy surface against his fingertips. "I will, baby. Just tell me."

With his thumb on Brynn's clit and his fingers inside, Paul fucked her slowly. Too slowly for Brynn to come, but enough to keep her on the razor's edge of orgasm. Brynn clenched the sides of the bathtub until her knuckles turned white, straining to come with Paul's slight touch. But Paul had known her long enough to know what it would take to push her over. He held back, waiting and aching with his own need.

"I've got all day, baby," he said, though every muscle in his body strained with rising tension. He couldn't deny Brynn—or himself—much longer. "Tell me what a beautiful, sexy girl you are."

Brynn gasped as Paul thumbed her clit hard. "Yes, god, yes, I'm beautiful," she moaned. "I'm so fucking beautiful. Fuck me, please fuck me."

"That's it," Paul coaxed, stroking her in earnest now. "My sexy girl."

"Sexy," Brynn repeated. "Fuck me, fuck your beautiful girl. I'm so hot, fuck me."

"Yes baby, yes," Paul said.

He fucked Brynn hard, harder than he intended, but Brynn didn't seem to mind at all. In fact, Brynn gripped his wrist and guided him, clamping her thighs around his hand. Paul could barely move his fingers inside Brynn, so he concentrated on rubbing her swollen clit. With just a few more rough strokes, he felt her thighs tighten convulsively around his hand as she started coming.

Brynn's body went taut and still, her hair loose around her shoulders now as she arched her back and pressed down on Paul's hand. Then she opened her mouth and let out a moan that rose to echo off the bathroom walls. Months of pent-up emotion and suppressed desire exploded from her in that scream. It was like watching a mythical banshee unleashed, and Paul could only watch and marvel at her beauty.

Wiggling his fingers inside her, he kept the pressure on her clit and rode out her orgasm. He stared at Brynn, as sexy as any woman he'd ever seen—coming, because of him. *For* him.

Brynn's orgasm seemed to last for minutes, and she gasped and panted as if she were in labor. Paul's heart nearly stopped at that thought, but Brynn showed no signs of pain—only pleasure so intense Paul felt like they had never shared anything quite like this before.

Finally, slowly, the moans faded to soft whimpers, and Brynn's eyes fluttered open. Her radiant smile was a sight to behold, and Paul forgot all about his own barely controlled desire. He'd done this—he had made Brynn smile like this.

Brynn opened her mouth, started to say something, and then shook her head. "Wow."

They both laughed, Paul's fingers still inside Brynn, most of the bath water on the tile floor. Brynn shivered and grimaced as she tried to sit up. Paul gently slid his cramped fingers free.

"Are you all right? Did I hurt you?" he asked, feeling a pang of remorse. Maybe he shouldn't have pushed Brynn so hard.

Brynn laughed. "Did you mean it?"

"What?"

"That I'm beautiful like this."

Paul ran a finger over the light purple mark that ran down Brynn's rounded belly. "Every inch of you, every curve, every mark. You're the most beautiful woman I've ever seen."

"I believe you." Brynn covered Paul's hand on her stomach. "Now get me out of this tub and take me to bed so you can fuck me properly."

Paul grinned. "Anything you want, beautiful."

# DAWN CHORUS

## Nikki Magennis

Of course it's not possible to stuff an entire duck-down pillow into the small shell-shaped hole of one's ear, but John was trying nonetheless. Not that cotton and duck feathers would be enough of a muffler. He doubted that pouring cement in his ears, wrapping his head in deep pile carpet, and lead-lining the walls would be enough.

The thump of the bass was the worst—he could feel it vibrate in the marrow of his bones—that regular, predictable bludgeoning kick. Pounding through the floor, rattling the glass in the window frames, making his whole body throb with a surround-sound headache. And then that jarring, jangling noise. Just after the out-of-tune wailing of the third chorus. He didn't know the title, but he knew the song by heart—every riff, lick, and drum roll.

She played it over and over. Usually at night. Always too loud. John ground his teeth so hard his jaw hurt. He glared at the glowing numbers on his bedside alarm clock. 3:10. Late enough to make him weep. He pressed his face into the mattress and moaned.

Tears brimmed in Jane's eyes as she sang along to the crackling LP. God, this song made her feel inside out. She played it loud with the window open, and the night air streamed into her studio flat, the dark breeze catching papers and spilling the unopened letters over the table, ruffling the edges of fabric, lifting the hem of the dresses hanging from the clothes rail, making the candles flicker and splutter with black, sooty flames.

She screwed up the volume another notch and walked to the open window.

"God, can you hear that?" she said, into the night. "Isn't it beautiful? Doesn't it make you want to fucking cry?"

John's suit hung over the back of his bedroom door. It wasn't pressed, but as a well-cut suit it would pass if he left it undisturbed until morning to let gravity pull out the creases.

It was not worth putting it on to go and visit his fiendish neighbor. It was not a good time for visiting. Nor, he thought bleakly, was it a good time for her to dig out her Mexican rock-and-roll LPs. Which she was in the process of doing, by the sound of it. He listened to her clunk and clatter. He sighed.

There was little else in his room apart from his bed, the suit, and the alarm clock. John preferred to live with as few possessions, as few distractions as possible. He'd spent a great deal of time stripping back and reducing and simplifying. His life should be—would be—empty of clutter and open to the fabulous array of small, quotidian noises that he so loved, were it not for the amplified car crash below him.

His nights were stuffed full, ripped apart and crammed with overbearing noise. Not just the music, either. The histrionics in between disturbed him greatly. She shook things loose in his head—distracting things like anger and resentment and a dumbstruck, confounded desire to saw his own ears off. These unpleasant emotional stirrings kicked around in his head like the hated bass beat.

Four hours, he thought. If he could make it through another four hours, he could get up and snort coffee and escape to the peaceful cell of his office.

Only now he was angry.

The monstrous hormone-riddled hysteric downstairs was howling, with her throaty, rough-honey voice, and bombs were going off inside John's head. He imagined drilling holes in the floor, shooting a fire extinguisher through her letterbox, tying her up and forcing her to listen to Brahms at 100 decibels.

He could call the police. They rarely showed up in this neck of the woods and would hardly bother for a minor neighborly row, not unless there were firearms involved—and John didn't have any on hand. Probably a good thing, overall.

Downstairs, the music paused. John took a deep breath. Silence crept into his ears like an old friend.

And then it was the Moaning Young Men, as John referred to them in his head. The song was called "Last Night Love." Or if you looked at it another way, the very last fucking straw, and the thing that was enough to make a usually calm and placid man roll out of bed and land on the floor with a resounding thud that would have alarmed an average human being but made no difference whatsoever to the noise freak below him.

Insouciant, juvenile guitar riffs accompanied John as he pulled up his loose-fit pajama bottoms and made for the door. Outside, the sound echoed tinnily in the stairwell, and John, shrinking under the fluorescent tube lights, cursed the fact he'd so far failed to make it out of the ghetto and anywhere near the hillside monastic retreat wreathed in majestic clouds that he so often dreamed of. Or the suburbs, even.

The concrete steps were cold underfoot, but he hardly noticed. He was trying not to listen to the voice in his head that had started its familiar old chant—the litany of injustices and everyday atrocities that had appalled him from his earliest awareness, through an offhand adolescence and his silent, thoroughly desperate early adulthood.

The music grew in volume as John's ego raved and ranted, taunting him with visions of the sleep-deprived misery he'd have to face the next day, so that by the time he arrived at the downstairs flat's door, he was ready to curl up his fist and pummel his future into submission.

What would he do? Could he overcome his habitual kindness and tendency to gracious politesse and make some pithy, outraged statement? He might swear at her. Yes, he might. John knocked, hard.

Four minutes later, he knocked again.

After a quarter of an hour freezing his feet outside a blank, unresponsive door, John climbed the stairs with the Moaning Young Men chasing after, mocking his hunched back. There were dark stars in his eyes now, the marks of growing rage of a man who, since he'd left the womb, had spent his life trying to recreate that sense of perfect, balanced stasis.

Back in his flat, he wanted to tear the place apart. But he lacked furniture to deconstruct. He looked at the window and thought about smashing it. Throwing the unwatched TV through it and watching it shatter over the rusting old fire escape.

A thought appeared in his mind, simple and frighteningly tempting.

It sent a shiver down his spine and made his mouth twitch. Before he could change his mind, he had crossed to the window and pulled it open, wide enough to clamber out onto the steel mesh platform.

The air was a wonderful shock, gripping him in a dark, oily embrace that somehow, instead of sobering him up, spurred him on.

He climbed gingerly down the staircase, flinching at the cold metal teeth digging into the soles of his bare feet, and came to a halt outside her window.

There. She was sitting at the table, her chin on her hand, face turned toward him, eyes closed as she nodded along with the music. John lifted his hand to knock. For a split-second, he paused, looking at the little detail he could see in the dim light of the interior. Half a dozen candles burned on a plate at her elbow, their gold flames casting soft little shadows on her face. She wore a loose kimono-type garment, something that shone a little and fell from her shoulders. She looked like a painting, he thought.

He shook his head. Waited for the pause in the song, the one he knew cut in after the middle eight. But instead of rapping on the glass, he found himself slamming it with his open hand, hard.

Jane jerked fully awake. The dark shape at the window flung itself onto her consciousness like a slap in the face. Instinctively, she reached for the empty plate beside her, scrabbling through dry crumbs before her fingers closed over the handle of the fork.

She raised it in front of herself like an undersized trident. Where was her phone? She had to get up and find it, but her eyes were fixed on the figure that hovered outside—a black shadow against the nearly black sky. He knocked on the window.

Jane frowned. If he wanted to break in and rape, rob and kill her, why was he knocking? She peered into the gloom. Was he wearing pajamas? The figure shifted as she looked at him, and she saw him wave a kind of salute.

Her neighbor? Yes, as she moved closer to the window, letting the hand holding the fork drop to her side, she thought there was something familiar about the shape of the man out there. The hair, normally brushed soft and falling over his face, stuck up wildly in all directions. But the broad, slightly stooped shoulders were his. And yes, as the candlelight fell on his scowling face, she recognized that resentful expression.

She took the last few steps confidently and pulled up the sash as though she often received visitors via the window.

"Either you're recreating *Breakfast at Tiffany's* or you locked yourself out," she said, her voice warm with relief. He could be a psychopathic weirdo, but he'd always seemed an almost ludicrously polite man, one of those monochromatic shadows that skirt around the edge of life. If she passed him on the stairs, he'd flatten himself against the wall and murmur a greeting she could hardly hear.

"Tiffany's?" he said, screwing his eyes up. He shook his head. "Your music."

Jane glanced at the stereo, still warbling away. "Oh, the music," she said, turning to give Mr. Pajamas a broad smile. "Siren song, huh? Come on in!"

"I..." John hesitated, and then he nodded and followed the sweep of her arm. He felt somehow compelled. He folded his tall frame and slipped through the gap into Jane's bedroom and stood on her Afghan rug holding his hands out as though feeling for invisible obstacles.

He was tall, Jane noticed. Maybe that was why he stooped. And he was blushing too—god, how long had it been since she saw a man blush! It lit up his face under the silvery stubble.

"Have a seat," she said, waving at the futon in the center of the room. "Want a drink?"

Before John could answer, she was sweeping over to the

sideboard and picking up the gin. She poured a generous tumblerful.

"I'm really not here to drink," he said.

"Oh, you'll need a locksmith, won't you? I'll get the Yellow Pages," she said and hustled to the bookshelves in the kitchen. She swiped an extra glass while she was there—at least now she didn't feel like such a lush. Drinking alone was not good for her soul. When she came back, John was sitting on the futon, looking thoughtful. She dropped the directory in his lap and raised her glass.

"Cheers, anyway," she said.

He sat and stared, his dark, ragged, sleepless eyes fixed on a point just to the left of her head.

"So what do they call you?" she said, ducking her head toward the empty air where his gaze was stuck. He looked down at the floor and cleared his throat.

"John," he said. "My name is John."

Jane nodded. "I'm Jane," she said, holding out a hand. "Nice to meet you."

They shook hands, and Jane held his cool, dry palm in her own. There was apparently something intensely interesting just behind her shoulder—his eyes kept sliding over there. Curious. But she took the chance to get a good look at him.

He had delicate water-blue eyes with lashes as long as a giraffe's. A stubble shadow that roughened his face and darkened the fine-carved bones of his jaw. Under his striped pajamas, his body was long and a little awkward, as though he didn't know where to put his limbs. He must be a bookseller, Jane thought. Something serious and elegant. She checked out his hands. Pale, fine, no rings. Yes, she thought, as she watched his face blotch with an awkward, patchy blush. He's lovely.

*Oh God,* John thought. *Oh sweet, gentle Jesus.* There was

a square framed picture of a tropical beach on the wall behind her head—an old record cover—and he carefully examined it. Otherwise he might look at her again. She was splashing more wine into her glass, and there was a faint purple stain on her top lip, but he couldn't help himself, his gaze was pulled down to the pulse at her throat, to the pale skin....

"Is everything okay?" she asked.

John let out a deep breath. "Your—shirt," he said. "It's not. It's undone."

"Huh?" Jane looked down to where the thin fabric of her blouse clung precariously to her jutting breasts. *And the breeze from the open window*, John said to himself. *Please God, help me.*

"'I'm trying not to look!" he blurted at last, shoving a hand into his hair and shaking his head. "I don't even know what I'm doing here. What am I doing here?" he murmured to himself. It felt like he was sleepwalking, like all the anger had pooled out of him and left him sitting here limp and foolish on this woman's couch.

Only, he realized with a growing, unnerving feeling like the swoop of his stomach as the roller coaster approaches the steep curve, not *all* of him was limp. His prick was starting to rise, reaching inexorably toward the light and poking rudely to attention. *No no no*, he told himself, but the brain in his dick just shrugged.

The flimsy cotton pajamas rose like a marquee being erected.

He grabbed the Yellow Pages and flapped them open in his lap. The sudden jolt made his cock leap joyfully and butt against the spine. He pressed the heavy book down and chanced a furtive glance at the girl. Jane.

"Hey," she said, swinging her hips gently from side to side.

"Yes?" He sounded like he was in pain.

"Dance with me," said Jane, and held out her hand. "I love this song."

John frowned.

"Come on, baby," Jane said, clicking her fingers in the air in front of his downturned face.

John raised his head, and his face was full of scrambled signals. His eyebrows twitched, and his cheeks flared. He shook his head harder.

"This song," he said at last, "is shit. This song and the next song, and the one when you flip the record over and crank up the volume on your terrible crackling speakers."

Jane took a step back, stunned. She reached for her throat. "You don't like it?"

"I don't like it," John said, tossing the Yellow Pages onto the couch and rising up. The cords of his pajamas swayed either side of his huge, angry erection, but he was beyond caring. "No. I don't like the crass verse, melody or chorus. I don't like sitting up all night listening to you croon and cackle and weep into your pillow..."

Jane's blue eyes pricked. She scrubbed at them roughly with the back of her hand.

"...I don't like lying in bed running through the ways I could short out the power in your flat or slip sleeping tablets into your water supply or set fire to my own flat and claim the insurance and have enough to move away somewhere I would never..."

John took a step forward. He was a good foot taller than Jane, but she'd never really noticed until now. He leaned in so close Jane could see the candle flames reflected in his eyes.

"...*ever* have to hear your infantile, pox-ridden, crapulous gutter music for the rest of my life."

Jane, the girl who had spent her life in a shouting match with the universe, suddenly went quiet. She looked up at John's dilated pupils. His fists hung by his sides, clenching and unclenching. Between them, his moderate but obvious erection waved gently back and forth like a conductor's baton.

She bit her lip. Covered her eyes with her hand. When she started shaking, John reached out and nearly touched her, but he couldn't do that, wouldn't do that. Had he scared her? If he held her now it would make it worse. Invade her space. He couldn't.

"Oh God," he said, "I'm sorry."

Jane made a stifled, uncertain noise.

John blew air through his pursed lips, gritted his teeth, and grabbed her shoulders. Immediately, her knees buckled, and she sank into his arms. John tried to maneuver his cock out of the way, but it kept insinuating itself between them.

"Jesus, I didn't mean to frighten you," John said, placing a hand lightly on the back of her bowed head. He could smell her hair. Bubblegum and cigarette smoke. She shook in his arms, and the movement made him doubly uncomfortable.

Jane pulled her face out from where it nestled in John's armpit. Smudged mascara had given her black-ringed panda eyes, but they were dry. She grinned.

"Frighten me? Unlikely, mister. John."

Her mouth—satin and juicy and soft and tender—was so close he could feel her breath on his face. She blurred in front of his eyes, and he thought it must be a mirage, that there was no way she would be moving in so close to him, bringing herself close enough to...

His world went suddenly sweet and upside down. Her lips on his. The tip of her tongue darted into his mouth. He thought to himself, *Oh!*

She was rubbing up against him. That devious cock of his

reared up against Jane's belly with delight, surging forward to meet her with bold joy and god-damn-whoa lust that made his heart ache.

They collapsed together, falling against the couch and scrabbling not to break the embrace. John's pajamas were a flimsy barrier, and Jane had his cock extricated and standing proud within seconds. In turn, John plucked at her kimono, pushed it roughly aside to free her breasts. He squeezed tenderly, leaning down to suckle and bite, but not hard enough to bruise.

"Yes," said Jane, "more, please more." He looked up and caught sight of the clock behind her head, just to the left of the framed record cover.

Five A.M. Dawn was starting to turn the sky light. His neighbor's tits were in his face, her nipples still wet from his mouth, and the music. The music was still playing.

"Excuse me," John said, and laid Jane down gently on the couch. He padded over to the stereo, trying to cover his awkward hard-on while Jane sighed behind him.

"What are you doing?" she asked, as he lifted the needle from the record and cut the singer off in midchorus.

Silence bloomed between them. John met her eyes, saw the restless spark and the tiredness in them. He moved to her and sank onto his knees in front of the couch.

"You love music," he murmured, whispering now as the quiet boomed in his ears. Jane nodded as he pulled her jeans open and bared her pubic hair, the top of her clit.

"So lie back," John said, lowering his head. "And listen."

He put his mouth to her, bending like a monk in prayer. The nerves in Jane's body all rushed between her legs, every fiber and pore of her pricked and readied for his touch. And he was quick. His tongue slid between her lips with delicate precision.

Should she have guessed? Someone who danced at the edges

of life, who flattened himself against walls to keep from brushing against her?

*Yes,* she thought as she closed her eyes and let out a deep breath. That supple, skillful mouth working against her now, that flicking and licking and sucking. Only a quiet man could be that good. Only someone who listened, who was sensitive to the minute ebb and flow of things.

Without the bath of music she was used to, her ears reached out to find the smaller noises. In the gap of silence, she heard a new tiny, intimate melody, so unfamiliar it was nearly embarrassing. There were only the wet sounds of him eating her. The creak of the futon spring under the weight of their swaying, rocking bodies. And her own ragged breath, quickening, rising to meet his silent intent.

She wound her hands into his hair. "Come up here," she said quietly.

He nodded, gave her pussy one last loud smacking kiss, and slid up and over her body, like he was polishing the curves of a cello with his own skin.

"Make love to me," she whispered. All the joy and angst of the night was melting under the dry heat of his body, the pleasant digs of his bones, and the scrabble of his hair against her own softer, smoother flesh. She let out a sigh, and the breath made her body give a little, made space for him to slip inside her.

John offered his cock to her, sliding it gracefully over the mouth of her slit and into her hot wet drum. As he did so, they locked eyes. "Jane," he said.

"Yes."

He plunged into her, fucked her with a decisiveness that took his own breath away. He fucked her enthusiastically but artlessly, his hips moving in time with the silent tick of the alarm clock upstairs that he couldn't see, bucking in again and again and again as if he couldn't help himself.

"Oh, oh, oh," she said, each time.

John lifted his head. He took a deep breath and smiled. He knew better.

He broke the rhythm. Paused, so that they could beat softly against one another—hear each other's pulse and tremor. Her body echoed his. Outside, a blackbird shrieked.

"Don't stop," she said, "I could do this forever."

"Yes," he said, pushing. "At least, with breaks in between to do other things."

"No," she said, "just fucking."

He held back. "You don't want me to kiss you, maybe?" His lips danced over hers. "Like that?"

"Okay," she said, nuzzling at him, nipping at his lower lip. "That too. But more of the fucking, also."

"Counterpoint?" he said, eating her mouth and starting, slowly, to fuck her again.

She laughed into his open mouth, let the laugh tumble into a groan.

"And more," he whispered, sliding a finger between them and rubbing at the key of her clit with the polished skill of a musician. "Like this. Glissando."

She responded, collecting him with her legs, heels, gathering him in, crying out, moaning, saying "Yes" and "Fuck" and the other crude, repetitive words that love songs are made of. Saying them over and over, making them sound soft with her lust-heavy tongue.

"Oh god. Fuck, I'm coming," she said, and he thought it sounded like a snatch of verse from one of her interminable records.

His cock contracted in response. A frown passed over his face. Jane's hips rose and fell, jerking with the release of orgasm.

Unable to hold back any longer, he spilled into her, uncontrolled, inelegant, probably making some inhuman noises of his own.

As they rocked together afterward, soothing the tremors, she kept murmuring her invocations, her vulgar litanies. "Fuck. Oh god. Oh, baby."

He raised his eyebrows. Tilted his head to hear her say them again. At last, he nodded. "Okay," he said. "Yes. And, I think, encore."

Outside, the birds started to sing; a glass-throated robin and a chattering wren joining the blackbird, then the chaffinch adding a plump trill and the other unnamed birds calling over each other, making the back garden a tangle of different voices.

By the time Jane came a second time the morning was a riot of beautiful, chaotic noise.

**SHAYLA BLACK** (aka Shelley Bradley) is the *New York Times* bestselling author of over 30 sizzling contemporary, erotic, paranormal, and historical romances for multiple print and electronic publishers. She has won or placed in over a dozen writing contests, including Passionate Ink's Passionate Plume, Colorado Romance Writers Award of Excellence, and the National Reader's Choice Awards. *Romantic Times* has awarded her Top Picks, a KISS Hero Award, and a nomination for Best Erotic Romance.

**RACHEL KRAMER BUSSEL** (rachelkramerbussel.com) is the editor of more than forty anthologies, including *Obsessed, Passion, Orgasmic,* and *Fast Girls.* She is senior editor at *Penthouse Variations* and writes a column for *SexIs* magazine. She covers sex, dating, and pop culture for a variety of publications and blogs at lustylady.blogspot.com and cupcakestakethecake. blogspot.com.

Award-winning author **ANGELA CAPERTON** writes eclectic erotica that challenges genre conventions. Look for her stories published with Black Lace and eBury Publishing, Circlet, Cleis Press (including *Best Women's Erotica 2010*),

Drollerie, eXtasy, Renaissance, Side Real Press, Xcite Books, and in the indie magazine *Out of the Gutter*. Visit her at blog.angelacaperton.com.

**HEIDI CHAMPA** has been published in numerous anthologies, including *Best Women's Erotica 2010*, *Playing with Fire*, *Frenzy*, and *Ultimate Curves*. She has also steamed up the pages of *Bust* magazine. If you prefer your erotica in electronic form, she can be found at Clean Sheets, Ravenous Romance, Oysters and Chocolate, and The Erotic Woman. Find her online at heidichampa.blogspot.com.

On her own and with coauthors, **ANDREA DALE** (www.cyvarwydd.com) has sold two novels to Virgin Books UK and approximately one hundred stories to Harlequin Spice, Avon Red, and Cleis Press, among others. A romantic at heart, she's a firm believer in second glances and second chances.

**SYLVIA DAY** is the national bestselling, award-winning author of more than a dozen novels and numerous short stories. Her work has been translated into several languages, and she's been honored with the *Romantic Times* Reviewers' Choice Award and multiple finalist nominations for Romance Writers of America's prestigious RITA® Award of Excellence.

**DELILAH DEVLIN** (DelilahDevlin.com) is an author of erotic romance and has a rapidly expanding reputation for writing deliciously edgy stories with complex characters. Whether creating dark, erotically charged paranormal worlds or richly descriptive westerns that ring with authenticity, Delilah Devlin "pens in uncharted territory that will leave the readers breathless and hungering for more...."

**KATE DOMINIC** is a former technical writer who now writes about much more interesting ways to put a Tab A into Slot B (or C or D). She is the author of more than three hundred short stories and is currently researching hot new settings for stories.

**JUSTINE ELYOT** is a multipublished author of erotica and erotic romance whose work has been published by Black Lace, Cleis Press, Xcite Books, Total E-Bound, Noble Romance, and Carina Press. Her titles include *On Demand, The Business of Pleasure,* and *Erotic Amusements,* and her fourth erotic novel, *Meeting Her Match* will be published in early 2012. She lives on the south coast of England.

**EMERALD**'s erotic fiction has been published in anthologies edited by Violet Blue, Rachel Kramer Bussel, Jolie du Pre, and Alison Tyler. She is an advocate for sexual freedom, reproductive choice, and sex worker rights, all topics she blogs about on her website, www.thegreenlightdistrict.org. Honey is one of her favorite foods.

**EROBINTICA** is the sex-obsessed persona of writer and poet Robin Elizabeth Sampson. She's had stories included in *Coming Together: Al Fresco* and in *Eat Me: Seven Stories of Gluttony.* Her poetry made the 2010 Seattle Erotic Art Festival and she has read at Philadelphia's Erotic Literary Salon. Her blog is erobintica.blogspot.com.

**SHANNA GERMAIN** grew up with clover, fence fixers, and wild horses. She still dreams of riding a bucking bronco. Visit her at www.shannagermain.com.

**NIKKI MAGENNIS** is a Scottish author and artist. She loves loud music, but only when she's in charge of the volume control. Find her short fiction in more than twenty anthologies from Cleis Press, Harlequin Spice, and others. Her erotic novels are published by Virgin Black Lace. Read more at nikkimagennis. blogspot.com.

**KATE PEARCE** graduated from the University College of Wales with an honors degree in history. She is a member of Romance Writers of America and is published by Kensington Aphrodisia, NAL Signet Eclipse, Ellora's Cave, Cleis Press, and Virgin Black Lace/Cheek.

**CRAIG J. SORENSEN**'s erotic stories have appeared in collections and periodicals worldwide. He currently resides in Pennsylvania, where he writes computer code by day and stories by night and early morning. Visit him at just-craig.blogspot.com.

**DONNA GEORGE STOREY** is the author of *Amorous Woman*, a steamy novel about an American woman's love affair with Japan. Her short fiction has appeared in *Passion: Erotic Romance for Women, Alison's Wonderland*, and *Best Women's Erotica*. Read more of her work at DonnaGeorgeStorey.com.

**SASKIA WALKER** is a British author whose erotica appears in more than seventy anthologies. Her novels include *Rampant, Inescapable*, and *The Harlot*. Saskia lives with her real-life hero, Mark, and a houseful of stray felines in the north of England, where she spends her days happily spinning yarns.

# ABOUT THE EDITOR

Described by *The Romance Reader* as "a budding force to be reckoned with," **KRISTINA WRIGHT** (www.kristinawright. com) is an author, editor, and college instructor. She has edited the Cleis Press anthologies *Fairy Tale Lust: Erotic Fantasies for Women*; *Dream Lover: Paranormal Tales of Erotic Romance*; *Steamlust: Steampunk Erotic Romance,* and her forthcoming anthologies include *Lustfully Ever After: Fairy Tale Erotic Romance* and *Duty and Desire: Military Erotic Romance for Women*. Her first anthology, *Fairy Tale Lust: Erotic Fantasies for Women,* was nominated for a Reviewers' Choice Award by *RT Book Reviews* and was a featured alternate of the Doubleday Book Club. Kristina's erotica and erotic romance fiction has appeared in more than eighty-five print anthologies, including *With This Ring, I Thee Bed; Bedding Down: A Collection of Winter Erotica; Nice Girls, Naughty Sex*; three editions of *Best Women's Erotica*; four editions of *Best Lesbian Erotica*; six editions of the *Mammoth Book of Best New Erotica,* and the erotic romance collections *Seduction, Liaisons,* and *Sexy Little Numbers*. She received the Golden Heart Award for Romantic Suspense from Romance Writers of America for her first novel *Dangerous Curves*. Her work has also been featured in the nonfiction guide *The Many Joys of Sex Toys* and magazines and ezines such as *Clean Sheets*, *Good Vibes*, *Libida*, *The Fiction Writer*, *The Literary Times*, *Scarlet Letters*, *The Sun,* and *The Quill*. Her nonfiction essay "The Last Letter" is included in the epistolary anthology *P.S. What I Didn't Say: Unsent Letters to Our Female Friends,* and her articles, interviews, and book reviews have appeared in numerous publications, both print and online. She is a member of Romance Writers of America as well as the RWA special interest chapters, Passionate Ink and Fantasy, Futuristic and Paranormal. She is a book reviewer for the Erotica Readers and Writers Association (erotica-readers. com) and the book club moderator for *SexIs* magazine's Naked Reader Book Club (nakedreaderbookclub.com). She holds degrees in English and humanities and teaches English composition and world mythology at the community college level. Originally from South Florida, Kristina has lived up and down the east coast with her husband, Jay, a lieutenant commander in the Navy. They welcomed the addition of their sons Patrick in December 2009 and Lucas in September 2011.

# More from Kristina Wright

**Buy 4 books, Get 1 FREE***

**Best Erotic Romance**
Edited by Kristina Wright

This year's collection is the debut of a new series!
"Kristina is a phenomenal writer...she has the enviable
ability to tell a story and simultaneously excite her
readers." —Erotica Readers and Writers Association
ISBN 978-1-57344-751-5   $14.95

**Steamlust**
*Steampunk Erotic Romance*
Edited by Kristina Wright

"Turn the page with me and step into the new worlds...where airships rule the skies,
where romance and intellect are valued over money and social status, where lovers boldly discover each other's bodies, minds and hearts." —from the foreword by
Meljean Brook
ISBN 978-1-57344-721-8   $14.95

**Dream Lover**
*Paranormal Tales of Erotic Romance*
Edited by Kristina Wright

Supernaturally sensual and captivating, the stories in *Dream Lover* will fill you with
a craving that defies the rules of life, death and gravity. "...A choice of paranormal
seduction for every reader. All are original and entertaining." —*Romantic Times*
ISBN 978-1-57344-655-6   $14.95

**Fairy Tale Lust**
*Erotic Fantasies for Women*
Edited by Kristina Wright

Award-winning novelist and erotica writer Kristina Wright goes over the river and
through the woods to find the sexiest fairy tales ever written. "Deliciously sexy action to make your heart beat faster." —Angela Knight, the *New York Times* bestselling
author of *Guardian*
ISBN 978-1-57344-397-5   $14.95

# Fuel Your Fantasies

**Carnal Machines**
*Steampunk Erotica*
Edited by D. L. King

In this decadent fusing of technology and romance, outstanding contemporary erotica writers use the enthralling possibilities of the 19th-century steam age to tease and titillate.
ISBN 978-1-57344-654-9  $14.95

---

**The Sweetest Kiss**
*Ravishing Vampire Erotica*
Edited by D.L. King

These sanguine tales give new meaning to the term "dead sexy" and feature beautiful bloodsuckers whose desires go far beyond blood.
ISBN 978-1-57344-371-5  $15.95

**The Handsome Prince**
*Gay Erotic Romance*
Edited by Neil Plakcy

A bawdy collection of bedtime stories brimming with classic fairy tale characters, reimagined and recast for any man who has dreamt of the day his prince will come. These sexy stories fuel fantasies and remind us all of the power of true romance.
ISBN 978-1-57344-659-4  $14.95

**Daughters of Darkness**
*Lesbian Vampire Tales*
Edited by Pam Keesey

"A tribute to the sexually aggressive woman and her archetypal roles, from nurturing goddess to dangerous predator."—*The Advocate*
ISBN 978-1-57344-233-6  $14.95

**Dark Angels**
*Lesbian Vampire Erotica*
Edited by Pam Keesey

*Dark Angels* collects tales of lesbian vampires, the quintessential bad girls, archetypes of passion and terror. These tales of desire are so sharply erotic you'll swear you've been bitten!
ISBN 978-1-57344-252-7  $13.95

# Red Hot Erotic Romance

### Obsessed
*Erotic Romance for Women*
Edited by Rachel Kramer Bussel

These stories sizzle with the kind of obsession that is fueled by our deepest desires, the ones that hold couples together, the ones that haunt us and don't let go. Whether just-blooming passions, rekindled sparks or reinvented relationships, these lovers put the object of their obsession first.
ISBN 978-1-57344-718-8   $14.95

---

### Passion
*Erotic Romance for Women*
Edited by Rachel Kramer Bussel

Love and sex have always been intimately intertwined—and *Passion* shows just how delicious the possibilities are when they mingle in this sensual collection edited by award-winning author Rachel Kramer Bussel.
ISBN 978-1-57344-415-6   $14.95

### Girls Who Bite
*Lesbian Vampire Erotica*
Edited by Delilah Devlin

Bestselling romance writer Delilah Devlin and her contributors add fresh girl-on-girl blood to the pantheon of the paranormal. The stories in *Girls Who Bite* are varied, un-expected, and soul-scorching.
ISBN 978-1-57344-715-7   $14.95

### Irresistible
*Erotic Romance for Couples*
Edited by Rachel Kramer Bussel

This prolific editor has gathered the most popular fantasies and created a sizzling, no-holds-barred collection of explicit encoun-ters in which couples turn their deepest desires into reality.
978-1-57344-762-1   $14.95

### Heat Wave
*Hot, Hot, Hot Erotica*
Edited by Alison Tyler

What could be sexier or more seductive than bare, sun-warmed skin? Bestselling erotica author Alison Tyler gathers explicit stories of summer sex bursting with the sweet eroticism of swimsuits, sprinklers, and ripe strawberries.
ISBN 978-1-57344-710-2   $15.95

# Love, Lust and Desire

**Red Velvet and Absinthe**
*Paranormal Erotic Romance*
Edited by Mitzi Szereto

Explore love and lust with otherworldly partners who, by their sheer unearthly nature, evoke passion and desire far beyond that which any normal human being can inspire.
ISBN 978-1-57344-716-4  $14.95

---

**In Sleeping Beauty's Bed**
*Erotic Fairy Tales*
By Mitzi Szereto

"Making their way into the spotlight again, Rapunzel, Little Red Riding Hood, Cinderella, and Sleeping Beauty, just to name a few, are brought back to life in Mitzi Szereto's delightful collection of erotic fairy tales."
—Nancy Madore, author of *Enchanted*
ISBN 978-1-57344-367-8  $16.95

**Foreign Affairs**
*Erotic Travel Tales*
Edited by Mitzi Szereto

"With vignettes set in such romantic locales as Dubai, St. Lucia and Brussels, this is the perfect book to accompany you on your journeys."
—*Adult Video News*
ISBN 978-1-57344-192-6  $14.95

**Pride and Prejudice**
*Hidden Lusts*
By Mitzi Szereto

"If Jane Austen had drunk a great deal of absinthe and slipped out of her petticoat... Mitzi Szereto's erotic parody of *Pride and Prejudice* might well be the result!"
—Susie Bright
978-1-57344-663-1  $15.95

**Wicked**
*Sexy Tales of Legendary Lovers*
Edited by Mitzi Szereto

"Funny, sexy, hot, clever, witty, erotic, provocative, poignant and just plain smart—this anthology is an embarrassment of riches."
—M. J. Rose, author of *The Reincarnationist* and *The Halo Effect*
ISBN 978-1-57344-206-0  $14.95

# Bestselling Erotica for Couples

**Sweet Life**
*Erotic Fantasies for Couples*
Edited by Violet Blue

Your ticket to a front row seat for first-time spankings, breathtaking role-playing scenes, sex parties, women who strap it on and men who love to take it, not to mention threesomes of every combination.
ISBN 978-1-57344-133-9 $14.95

---

**Sweet Life 2**
*Erotic Fantasies for Couples*
Edited by Violet Blue

"This is a we-did-it-you-can-too anthology of real couples playing out their fantasies." —Lou Paget, author of *365 Days of Sensational Sex*
ISBN 978-1-57344-167-4 $15.95

**Sweet Love**
*Erotic Fantasies for Couples*
Edited by Violet Blue

"If you ever get a chance to try out your number-one fantasies in real life—and I assure you, there will be more than one—say yes. It's well worth it. May this book, its adventurous authors, and the daring and satisfied characters be your guiding inspiration."—Violet Blue
ISBN 978-1-57344-381-4 $14.95

**Afternoon Delight**
*Erotica for Couples*
Edited by Alison Tyler

"Alison Tyler evokes a world of heady sensuality where fantasies are fearlessly explored and dreams gloriously realized."—Barbara Pizio, Executive Editor, *Penthouse Variations*
ISBN 978-1-57344-341-8 $14.95

**Three-Way**
*Erotic Stories*
Edited by Alison Tyler

"Three means more of everything. Maybe I'm greedy, but when it comes to sex, I like more. More fingers. More tongues. More limbs. More tangling and wrestling on the mattress."
ISBN 978-1-57344-193-3 $15.95

Ordering is easy! Call us toll free or fax us to place your MC/VISA order.
You can also mail the order form below with payment to:
Cleis Press, 2246 Sixth St., Berkeley, CA 94710.

## ORDER FORM

| QTY | TITLE | PRICE |
|-----|-------|-------|
| | | |
| | | |
| | | |
| | | |
| | | |
| | | |
| | | |
| | | |

SUBTOTAL _____

SHIPPING _____

SALES TAX _____

TOTAL _____

Add $3.95 postage/handling for the first book ordered and $1.00 for each additional
book. Outside North America, please contact us for shipping rates. California residents
add 8.75% sales tax. Payment in U.S. dollars only.

**\* Free book of equal or lesser value. Shipping and applicable sales tax extra.**

**Cleis Press • Phone: (800) 780-2279 • Fax: (510) 845-8001**
**orders@cleispress.com • www.cleispress.com**
**You'll find more great books on our website**

**Follow us on Twitter @cleispress • Friend/fan us on Facebook**